Microbiology! Because What You Don't Know Will Kill You

Alan H.B. Wu, Ph.D.

To: Waikiki Health

Abd

Aug 2011   Honolulu

Microbiology! Because what you don't know will kill you contain fictitious characters, events, and places. Any resemblance to actual persons, living or dead, business establishments, events, or locales is entirely coincidental. The science described in these stories, however, is factual.

ISBN-13: 978-0-989-3485-7-7
eBook ISBN: 078-0-989-3485-8-4

Dedication

This book is dedicated to my wife who continues to challenge me to achieve.

Acknowledgement

I thank Dr. Valerie Ng, Chair, Department of Pathology, Alameda County Medical Center/Hyland Hospital, Oakland, CA and Dr. Yvette McCarter, Director, Clinical Microbiology Laboratory, University of Florida, Jacksonville for their review of the manuscript.

Table of Contents

Prologue

There are certain truths within the physical world that are invariable. A ball that is dropped on earth will fall to the ground. A fire will cause oxidative damage to combustibles. There are also truths within the medical world. A tissue starved of oxygen will eventually die. Muscles that do not exercise will atrophy. Imagine a world where some of these truths change. There would be inconceivable chaos if gravity on earth became antigravity. Or if an engineer who is told that there is no longer a reaction for every action.

Yet, changes in medical truths occur within the science of clinical microbiology on a regular basis. A drug that is highly effective in eradicating a microorganism strain in one year can be completely ineffective the following year. Because a microorganism has a short life, there can be multiple generations that exist within just a few months. This results in the development of mutations that enable a strain to survive in the presence of broad-spectrum antibiotic use. As first described by Charles Darwin, "natural selection" causes evolutionary change. Alterations that favor the survival of an organism will have increased likelihood for survival and reproduction. Mutations that are not favorable, e.g., sensitivity of microorganisms towards antibiotics, will not self-perpetuate

It is the responsibility of the clinical microbiology lab to provide tools for diagnosis of infectious disease. This requires knowledge of how bacteria, viruses and parasites grow and how they can be destroyed. This becomes a difficult task for the clinical microbiologist, as these microorganisms mutate and evolve.

One way to combat this problem is not attempt to grow the bacteria on media, but examine the organism's genetic makeup. By sequencing the DNA or RNA of these organisms, one can identify the strain and its mutations. Another means termed serology, is to measure human antibodies that are raised against these bacteria and viruses during an infection. Even if a microorganism mutates, it is likely that the human body will still be stimulated to produce antibodies as a defense mechanism or response to an infection.

What these analytical techniques cannot do is determine which drugs will be effective or if the microorganism is alive and causing disease. Therefore a combination of genetic, serology, and cultures, where lab technologists attempt to grow these microorganisms onto favorable media, are needed.

This book is the third of a series of books focusing on the value of the clinical laboratory to the practice of medical science. As with the first two books, my involvement and that of the chemistry and microbiology laboratories in real clinical cases is highlighted. But instead of drugs and clinical laboratory tests, this book focuses on infectious diseases. As before, the names and places have been fictionalized to comply with privacy laws. This book contains more connections to the rich and illustrious history of clinical microbiology. This information is factual.

Pipetteman

Bronislaw was a Jewish child living in Eastern Europe in the 1940s and survived the Second World War and the Holocaust. After the war, he grew up behind the iron curtain in one of the Eastern bloc countries. Bronislaw's family was very poor. He was very thin when he was young and always hungry. Nevertheless, Bronislaw was not an unhappy child. He had a sharp mind and excelled in science. He was selected out of hundreds of thousands of candidates to enter medical school at the state academy directly after high school and eventually became a pathologist. Bronislaw devoted himself to the profession as he never married. He read many scientific journals and wished that his country had the financial resources that would allow him to conduct medical research studies in his country. But research and healthcare was not among the priorities of his government, so Bronislaw made plans to immigrate to the United States. Although he was a physician, he was not paid well and he had to save for many years before he could come to America. In the meantime, he wrote and became friendly with Dr. Magnar Amand, who was a professor of pathology at Johns Hopkins University, who emigrated from Europe 25 years earlier. Bronislaw found out that Dr. Amand was originally from his hometown. Through their letters, Dr. Amand took a liking to the young Bronislaw and agreed to sponsor his visa to the U.S. to work in his laboratory. Immigration was much easier in the 1970s than in the post-9/11 era. Bronislaw acquired the J-1 visa that enabled him to gain additional medical training and he was on his way to Baltimore.

Bronislaw worked in Dr. Amand's lab for several years doing medical research. After 1 year, he was offered a full time job which enabled him to obtain a green card as a permanent resident. This job was a life-long dream for him. He didn't miss his old previous occupation working as a pathologist. Bronislaw did ask about obtaining a medical license, but was told he would have to do a 4-year residency in pathology and laboratory medicine and a 1-year fellowship in order to practice in the U.S. By then he was in his late forties and was content being a research scientist. His English language skills were not great. In the research laboratory, he didn't have to speak in public.

All of this came to an abrupt end when Dr. Amand was involved in a tragic and fatal car crash outside of the Washington DC beltway area. With his death, Dr. Amand's federal research funding was removed and his research lab dismantled, so Bronislaw was out of work. Now in his early fifties, Bronislaw sought a more secure occupation than being a research scientist, so he entered a one-year medical technology training program. This enabled him to work in a clinical laboratory performing tests on patients. It was somewhat insulting to him that he had to go back to school because he had far more knowledge and experience in laboratory medicine than any of his instructors, but he bit his tongue and became a model student. His med tech classmates were 30 years younger. But they recognized that he had expertise in the area and regularly went to him for advice. He helped them with their lessons, while they helped him with his English. Upon graduation, Bronislaw easily passed the national board examination, became licensed by the American Society for Clinical Pathology, and found a job as a medical technologist and moved to Texas.

*

Bronislaw had been working at the General Hospital for many years when I landed my first job as the associate director of clinical chemistry, so he was one of the staff members that I inherited. Back 30 years ago, Bronislaw was assigned to the radioimmunoassay or "RIA" laboratory. Drs. Rosalyn Yalow and Solomon Berson discovered the RIA technique for measuring hormone concentrations in human blood. They discovered that antibodies raised in sheep and goats can be used as a reagent for capturing and detecting hormones circulating in blood. The two were awarded the 1977 Nobel Prize in Physiology or Medicine. Unlike the totally automated immunoassays of today, radioimmunoassay testing during the early years was performed by manual methods. Accurate and precise measurements required meticulous attention to detail. Within our clinical laboratory staff, Bronislaw became exceptionally skilled at performing this test. Word got around the General Hospital that if you wanted accurate thyroid hormone results, Bronislaw had to be in the lab that day. When learning that their patient's blood was not tested by Bronislaw, some physicians asked their patients to return to the clinic and to have their blood re-drawn so that it could be tested by our star technologist. When I heard about this practice,

I felt this was a waste of our resources but I could not change a doctor's lab ordering practices. So I went to see him to see why he was superior and to see if my other techs could be as proficient as he. As soon as I arrived, I saw something that shocked me and would later haunt Bronislaw.

*

An essential part of producing reliable clinical laboratory results is being able to deliver a precise volume of sample to the test tube. Because a microscopic amount of sample was needed, it was difficult to extract the same amount of fluid each time the test was performed. In the early 1980s, a "pipette" was used to remove a volume of sample. The pipette is a long hollow thin piece of glass designed to deliver a fixed volume of fluid. There is a line that is etched into the tube near the top that is used to precisely measure the amount of fluid needed. The tip of the pipette is placed into the serum sample. Gentle suction is applied at the top of the tube enabling fluid to be drawn into the tube, the same way that a straw is used to drink beverages. The individual stops the suctioning when the fluid level is above the graduated line but before it reaches the end of the tube. Normally, suction is provided by placing a squeezed rubber bulb on top of the tube and gently releasing the tension on the bulb. After removal of suction, the tech's index finger is placed on top of the tube to stop the flow of fluid out of the bottom. A gradual release of the finger causes the fluid to drip out and back into the original sample. When the level of the fluid inside the tube exactly reaches the graduated marked line, the finger is again placed over the tube stopping its flow. The pipette is withdrawn from the sample, the tip is wiped with a tissue, and the pipette is

4

placed into the measuring test tube. A release of the finger delivers the sample. As there is always some fluid left, positive pressure is applied at the top of the pipette to expel all remaining fluid.

Bronislaw was highly proficient in pipetting accuracy. Every year, the laboratory held a contest to see who can pipette with the highest reproducibility. The winner received a certificate and a button. Bronislaw won the contest almost every year. He wore his award buttons proudly on the lapel of his white laboratory coat. Most of the other techs thought it was comical that he took this contest so seriously and his obsession with winning every year.

In watching Bronislaw's laboratory technique, I was dumbfounded to see that he was mouth pipetting. Rather than using the bulb, he placed the tip of the pipette to his lips and aspirated the sample by sucking on the end of the tube. I immediately told him that this was a dangerous and unacceptable practice and asked him to stop immediately.

"Bronislaw, serum contains a lot of infectious and toxic agents," I told him in a stern voice and without hesitation. "Mouth pipetting unnecessarily exposes you to biological and chemical hazards. You are also setting a poor example for our younger technologists. I cannot allow you to continue this practice."

"I have been pipetting in this way since before you were in born. I am extremely careful and know the risk. I have never aspirated any sample into my mouth. I grew up in ghettos of Warsaw during the war. I have been exposed to every known infectious disease and have antibodies to prove it. I have not been sick for a day in my career," Bronislaw said proudly. Bronislaw thought to himself, I'll be damned if some kid is going to tell me how to perform a laboratory test! "Go away now and let me do my vork." Bronislaw had trouble pronouncing "W's".

Thinking that it was useless to argue with him, I quickly left the laboratory and headed straight to see the chief of laboratory services. To my surprise, not only did he know of this practice, but he himself practiced it years ago.

"We don't have a policy against mouth pipetting," he told me. "In our day, everybody pipetted that way. It is easier and faster. While we don't recommend it to anyone today, we leave it up to the individual technologist."

My next stop was the risk management department at the Hospital. They said the same thing; all policies and procedures are at the discretion of the department head. At the time, there were no laboratory regulations prohibiting this practice. I left the office but felt that more should be done. I was somewhat relieved to find out that Bronislaw was the only one in my staff who was practicing mouth pipetting. At least his lab habits are not rubbing off to anyone else, I thought.

*

Davy and Arturo was a gay couple living in an apartment near Montrose Street, just south of downtown Houston. While Davy was monogamous, Arturo would go to gay bars and have casual sex behind Davy's back. Within a few weeks, Arturo began to experience symptoms of the flu. He became fatigued, had a headache, and swollen glands. He thought he had caught a cold and took the usual cold medications. However, when his symptoms persisted, Davy took him to the General Hospital where he was admitted to the intensive care unit. Nobody from the ICU team could figure out what he suffered from. His doctor ordered a broad panel of blood tests including tests for mononucleosis, hepatitis A and B, and non-A and non-B. Hepatitis C was not discovered yet. Everything came up negative. Arturo's health declined dramatically. He developed a respiratory infection caused by the pneumocystis pneumonia fungus. His greatly weakened immune system caused this infection. He could not eat and was put on intravenous feeding. His face became pale and he lost a lot of weight. The doctors could not determine the cause and had no cure for Arturo. They thought his disease was communicable, so they put him in isolation. Within a few months of his hospital admission, Arturo passed away. Davy was devastated at losing his partner. He was not afraid of catching what Arturo had, and stayed by his side to the very end. Unfortunately, Davy himself would die from this same disease within a year. He was buried in a plot next to Arturo.

During Arturo's initial medical workup, my hormone laboratory received one of his blood samples for a thyroid stimulating hormone test. His doctors erroneously thought his lack of energy was due to hypothyroidism. Bronislaw was the technologist performing the test that day. He was in the process of mouth pipetting a sample of Arturo's blood when the fire alarm went off in the laboratory. It was one of our biannual drills. Although he had been through countless fire drills before, on this day, Bronislaw was startled by the loud sound. While distracted, the pipette tip came out of the blood sample while he was still sucking. This sudden change in the negative vacuum pressure caused him to aspirate some of Arturo's serum directly into Bronislaw's mouth. He put down the sample and the pipette and went over to the sink to spit the serum out. He then went to the drinking fountain and rinsed out his mouth thoroughly with water, spitting the water out into the sink. He repeated this process two more times. Satisfied, he didn't think any more of the incident and went back to work. Bronislaw didn't realize the significance of the open cold sore he had on the inside of his mouth that got exposed to Arturo's sample, however brief it was.

A few weeks later, Bronislaw began to suffer the same symptoms as Arturo. He had a mild fever and felt unusually tired. He didn't let it slow him down and initially, he didn't miss a day of work. Eventually, he became too sick to work and called for a sick day for the first time in years. After a week of absence, someone from the laboratory called him to see how he was doing. Bronislaw picked up the phone but his voice was very cracked and feeble. Fearing that he was really sick, we called an ambulance to go to his apartment. The emergency medical technicians saw that he was gravely ill and with his permission, immediately transported him to the General Hospital. Members of my staff came to visit him while he was in the ICU. They were shocked to see that Bronislaw's health had deteriorated in just a few weeks. Bronislaw was in and out of consciousness. When awake, we could tell through his eyes that he was appreciative of the visits from his colleagues in the lab but he could not speak. When he saw me, I sensed that he was sorry for what happened and that maybe the young professor was right. Within a few days, Bronislaw died. The cause of his death was listed as immune deficiency of unknown etiology. Most of the clinical laboratory attended his funeral. Someone brought his lab coat and left it in his coffin. Another coworker put one of the glass pipettes that Bronislaw used next to his body for burial. Our annual pipette contest was named in his honor, and the winner was taken out to lunch at an Eastern European restaurant off of Westheimer Road. It was a small token to keep his memory alive.

A few years later, Bronislaw was in one of my dreams. We were in a relay race and he is passing the baton to me to run the final leg. Except that instead of a baton, he was passing me a contaminated glass pipette. Horrified when I see this, I drop the baton and it falls to the ground and breaks. Perhaps I let him down by not insisting that he stop his mouth pipetting practice when I first learned of it. I am disturbed by his death for many years.

*

Bronislaw contracted an HIV infection from his exposure to Arturo's infected blood sample. They and tens of thousands of others with the same symptoms died in the early 1980s of acquired immune deficiency syndrome or AIDS. There was no cure or laboratory test available to diagnose AIDS. In 1983, Dr. Luc Montagnier and Francoise Barre-Sinoussi at the Pasteur Institute isolated the virus responsible for AIDS. A test was soon developed that is used to diagnosis infections. But it would be many years before effective antiviral treatment for HIV infection became available.

During the early HIV years, there was a significant hysteria regarding how the virus is transmitted. This fear led to an extreme shortage of students entering the field of medical technology. With anti-retroviral therapy, AIDS is no longer a fatal disease. One benefit of the HIV era is the adherence to safe laboratory procedures with discontinuation of mouth pipetting. Today, all samples are treated as capable of producing life-threatening infections. Given the dangers of blood, it is inconceivable today for anyone to perform pipetting by mouth. Moreover, pipettes in use today have spring loaded plungers that do not require any external suction. Personal protective equipment including lab coats, gloves, and eye protection are standard issue to all medical technologists today, with penalties for lack of compliance. There have been very few cases of HIV infection contracted by healthcare workers such as clinical laboratory technologists. Hepatitis B and C are considerably more infectious and accidents have led to more infections of healthcare workers.

The *Livermore*

The old man held his 7 year old great granddaughter Lucy on his lap. She reached up to touch the man's scarred face.

"How come your face is so rough granddaddy?" she asked. The old man was actually another generation beyond being her grandfather but it didn't matter.

"I don't really know, but it was because of this that I met granny," Gasten said pointing to his face as he spoke. Charles, Lucy's father, asked his grandfather if he was up to telling his story. Gasten had just arrived a few days earlier from England and was visiting Charles' family.

*

Gasten was born in Liverpool in 1905. His father worked for White Star, and he was among the hundreds of men who built the best luxury cruise ships of the day. From all accounts available, Gasten lived a normal infancy and young childhood. Then a series of events changed Gasten's destiny from normal to bizarre. When Gasten was 7, White Star's "unsinkable" liner that Gasten's father help build, sank in the North Atlantic. Many of Gasten's neighbors who worked on the maiden voyage perished in those icy north waters that night, unable to board one of the few lifeboats that were available. It was at this point that Gasten took an interest in cruise ships and his father's occupation. His father would sneak Gasten on to the worksite on weekends so the boy could see how the ship was constructed and the many services it offered to passengers. Gasten's interest might not have led him into this direction had the *Titanic* not hit an iceberg.

The boy's second catastrophic event was the death of his parents. The winter of Gasten's 12th year was particularly cold and wet in England. If he wanted to keep his job, his father had no choice but to work under harsh conditions, even when the temperatures and wind chill were well below the freezing point. His father's immune system wore down after weeks of hard work and he contracted pneumonia from a bacterial infection. Gasten's mother also contracted it from the father as they all lived in very close quarters. Gasten's parents died within a week of each other from the respiratory disease. It was fortunate and rather surprising that Gasten did not catch pneumonia from his parents. But because he did not have any living relatives, Gasten was moved to an orphanage near the shipyard.

Gasten adjusted well at first to his new environment. While living at the home, he developed an interest in music. He joined the orphanage's choir and sang in church every Sunday. Without any formal instructions, he learned how to play the piano and taught himself how to read and write music. The nuns who ran the orphanage were truly amazed at this boy's talent. Two years later, Gasten took a job as a delivery boy at White Star while still living at the orphanage. He was paid under the table because he and other boys from town who worked there were underage.

When Gasten was 15, the third major event of his live occurred. He came home from the shipyard after a day of work with a fever and a rash on his face. The nuns treated it with ointments and salts but to no avail. The rash became worse requiring hospitalization. Neither Gasten nor his doctor knew how he received this rash. When asked, the boy told his doctor and nurse that he had not been exposed to any chemical or solvents. This was a lie, but Gasten didn't want to lose his job at the shipyard. Gasten remained in the hospital for a few weeks and made a full recovery. But the right side of his face was scarred and he was disfigured. Many of the children at the orphanage teased him about his appearance and it caused Gasten to become withdrawn and reticent. He stopped singing in the choir but privately continued his interest in playing the piano when nobody was around and continued writing music.

About a year later, Gasten left the orphanage. He took most of his possessions but left no note as to his whereabouts. Gasten landed a job on the *Livermore* doing maintenance work below deck. The ship's management felt sorry for him because of his disfigurement. He was not allowed to interact with the passengers. When the ship was at sea, White Star took care of all of his living needs. He shared a room with other low-paying workers in the bowels of the ship. However, when the ship was docked, Gasten secretly stayed on board. None of the senior officers or executives of White Star knew he did this.

Then one day while at sea, a five year old girl named Ellie wandered away from her parents and accidently ran into Gasten. Upon seeing Gasten's face, the girl screamed in horror. The parents quickly ran to their child's aid only to find that the girl had calmed down and Gasten was waiting for the parents to return the child to them.

When they arrived, they were aghast. "Boy, who are you? What are you doing with our daughter?" The father demanded as he immediately took the child away from Gasten.

"I did nothing sir. She was wandering below deck and I wanted to return her to her parents," was Gasten's response.

Gasten's supervisor was nearby and heard the commotion. "What's going on here Gasten?"

Before the boy could respond, Ellie's father said, "This horrible boy lured my daughter below and was going to molest her."

"That's not true!" Gasten responded. But the supervisor was not listening.

"I demand that this boy be dismissed immediately, or I will contact the authorities and have him arrested for kidnapping, and charge White Star for negligence!" the Father shouted. He took Ellie's hand and started to walk away. As they were walking, Ellie turned her head back to look at Gasten again. There was no fear in her face.

When the ship returned to port, White Star with no other choice dismissed the teenager. Gasten had no place to go and was terrified. He didn't feel welcomed by the other children at the orphanage and he didn't have enough money to rent an apartment. So later that night, Gasten returned to the ship. He knew of a place deep down in the hull where rarely anybody goes. For many years thereafter, he secretly lived there as a permanent stowaway.

It was easy for Gasten to live on the ship undetected.

He knew nearly every inch of the boat and the daily routines when the ship was at sea. He had secret viewing points where he could see what was happening without being noticed. But he was not perverse nor a peeping Tom. Given the thousands of meals the ship served to its passengers and crew each day, it was not hard for Gasten to find food without attracting attention. When the ship was docked and only a skeleton crew was on board, Gasten snuck into the largely soundproof music room to compose and practice on the piano. Over the years, he composed several songs that nobody ever heard or knew about. The ship played small musicals for the passengers and had a troupe of singers and musicians.

*

Fifteen years passed and still Gasten remained undiscovered living on the liner. Life was very lonely for him, but he felt he had little choice because of his facial appearance and how people reacted when they saw him. Then one day, fate intervened again. To Gasten's amazement, Ellie, now a beautiful grown woman of 20, was auditioning for a part as a backup singer. Directly below the stage and hidden from view, Gasten heard the girl's audition. He thought that she had talent but could use some coaching. Ellie received the job as a backup singer and hired to sing on a few cruises that year.

For the next few weeks, Gasten secretly watched her rehearse with the group and when she sang alone after hours. He could see Ellie was really trying to improve. But she was getting nowhere because the show's director spent all of her time with the main diva. So Gasten decided that he would reveal himself to Ellie. But first, he needed to cover up the scars on the right side of his face. He went to the ship's machine shop and found a thin piece of sheet metal. He carefully cut, polished and molded the metal to the outline of his face. He drilled and fashioned a hole for his right eye to see. The work took days, but the piece fitted so perfectly that it did not require any adhesive or strap. He painted it to a bright glossy white. He put on black pants and shirt. The white mask was a sharp contrast to his dark clothing. Then he looked into the mirror and thought, *not bad. Not bad at all. This will do nicely.*

Gasten waited a few more weeks to gather the confidence for Ellie to see him. Finally, Gasten thought the time was right, and he made his move. She was alone when he sneaked into the rehearsal hall and hid behind a wall. When she sang, he sang along with her. When she heard another voice she was startled and stopped singing. Gasten continued on with the song for a few more bars and then stopped. It was like an echo. Ellie looked around and said, "Who's there? Is somebody there? Come on, I heard you. Show yourself."

That was Gasten's cue. He came out from behind the wall and shadow and into the light. It was the first time that anyone seen or spoken to him in over a decade. "Ellie, do you remember me? You were just a child when...."

Ellie interrupted him, "I know you. You, you're the one. I was a small girl then. I was afraid at first but then I realized you weren't going to hurt me. My father didn't understand." she said, looking down while remembering. Then after a pause, she came back to the present. "What are you doing here?"

"I'm here to help coach you. I've been watching you, and I think you could be the star of this show." Ellie was shocked

16

to hear that someone was secretly watching her. They were alone in a room thousands of miles at sea. She had no reason to distrust Gasten. If he was going to hurt her, he would have already. Gasten told her that if anybody found out about him, he would be removed from the ship. With his disfigurement, he had nowhere to go. So they formed a secret student-teacher bond. Gasten worked with Ellie each night for weeks. It seemed to pay off. She was getting better and more confident.

Ellie's break came during her second tour of cruises on the *Livermore*. During the middle of the cruise, the main singer became sick and developed laryngitis. The director wavered on cancelling of the show. Ellie protested claiming she knew all of the songs and asked if she could audition to fill the part. Reluctantly, the director let her sing. Gasten was hiding in his usual spot below the stage. As she began to sing, he was mouthed the words. Ellie was spectacular. The director felt she was as good if not better than their star. She was given the part. The audience loved her so much that when the main star recovered from her illness, she was demoted to be one of the chorus singers, the role that Ellie had. Gasten was overjoyed at the success of his pupil. He spent even more time with her and was falling in love. Ellie had some feelings towards Gasten too, but it was their secret. She wasn't sure if it was an infatuation or true love. She was only 21 years old. Ellie's father cheated on her mother a few years earlier, and they were divorced.

When her tour of duty was up, Gasten was sad to see Ellie leave. But he obtained her address and they wrote to each other regularly. When she signed up to perform the following cruise season, Gasten was overjoyed. *I'm going to ask her to marry*

17

me, he thought. But when she arrived, things had changed. During one of her on-shore gigs she met Spenser, a saxophone player who played in the show. They began dating. They told the director that they were married and shared the same cabin on board. Gasten was crushed. The boy was tall, young, and handsome. When he learned that they weren't actually married, he vowed to fight for her.

Gasten continued to coach Ellie on the ship without Spenser's knowledge. Spenser wondered why she would be gone for an hour at a time at night so he followed her. When he heard another man's voice through the door he broke into the room. "Who is this man?" he demanded.

"Spenser, what are you doing here? He is my coach," Ellie replied.

"You never told me about him." Then he saw Gasten's disfigurement. He pointed to it and said, "What's wrong with his face?"

Gasten made his move. "Go away boy, we are busy."

"How long has this been going on," Spenser demanded.

"Calm down, there is nothing between us," was Ellie's reply. But that was a lie. These last few weeks, Ellie was comparing Gasten to Spenser and found herself falling for the older masked man. He was more mature, kinder, and devoted. Ellie could see past Gasten's disability. Spenser, on the other hand, was annoying, immature and selfish.

"This is crazy. I won't put up with this. You have to choose. I won't be a second fiddle to a freak," Spenser said, stomping his foot and putting his hands on his hips.

Ellie had never seen such behavior in Spenser. She was

quickly concluding that Spenser was not the man of her dreams. "I won't be bullied by you," she said at last. "I will not choose. Please leave now. We have work to do."

"That does it, we're through. I am going to ask the director to move me in with the other musicians and at the first opportunity, I am leaving the ship."

"Fine! Get out!" Ellie shouted and turned her head away from Spenser and looked at Gasten.

Spenser slammed the door on his way out. Gasten was never more in love with Ellie than at that moment. Instead of rehearsing, they hugged and then he kissed her passionately. Ellie snuck Gasten into her room, and locked the door. He took off his mask and revealed himself to the girl. She was not horrified. Instead, they made love. It was his first time. Gasten fell asleep hugging her for the next few hours. Then, before she awoke, he slipped away, back to his hidden perch on the ship.

*

Lucy sat quietly throughout the whole story fascinated by every word her great grandfather said. Gasten married Ellie and they left the *Livermore* behind forever. He became a music director and Ellie had a successful stage career in London for many decades before they both retired to Liverpool.

Gasten paused for a moment thinking about Ellie and remembering how much he loved her. How much he still loved her. His eyes then focused on the young child and he said, "it's bed time for you pumpkin." Charles picked Lucy up, hugged her and took her up to her room.

Charles was a clinical microbiologist and a postdoctoral fellow in my laboratory. We give our students much flexibility as to the type of research studies that is conducted. Gasten never before spoke about his disfigurement to Charles or anyone in the family. Charles suspected that Gasten was inflicted by a flesh eating bacterium. While he was visiting, he convinced Gasten to undergo a medical examination.

"What can be done now after so many years?" Gasten wanted to know. Gasten had plastic surgery to repair his facial lesions and didn't wear the mask any longer but was still scarred.

"We have new tools that were not around back in your day. I am looking for a particular antibody that may still be present in your blood." Charles explained that the body's immune response to a foreign host can last many decades. The presence of these antibodies would indicate that he was exposed to a particular bacterium that caused his facial necrosis so many years earlier.

"Just before your rash appeared, did you suffer any injuries to your face, Grandpa?"

"Oh yes, working in a shipyard was hard work. I would occasionally bump into beams and pipes all the time," Gasten responded. Blood was collected from Gasten and sent to our lab. A few days later, we isolated IgG antibodies directed to a protein called "M1." From this, Charles concluded that the cause of his grandfather's facial disfigurement was due to a bacterial infection. He presented this case in our infectious disease rounds.

"My grandfather suffered from a necrotizing fasciitis caused by an infection with *Streptocccus pyogenes.*"

"Flesh-eating bacteria syndrome!" was the response by one of the medical students. Charles went on to describe the importance of the antibodies in the pathophysiology of the

20

disease.

"This is the same microorganism that is responsible for toxic shock syndrome," he concluded. While the science was interesting, his family's life story was much more fascinating to us.

A few months later, Charles and Lucy flew to Liverpool. Charles explained to Gasten what the cause for his facial injuries from so many years ago. Gasten nodded his head in agreement but didn't fully understand the medical explanation. Later that afternoon, Gasten asked Charles and his daughter to accompany him to a cemetery in Liverpool. This was where the remains of many victims of the *Titanic* disaster were buried. Ellie was there too. When they approached her headstone, Charles held Lucy's hand and took a step back to allow Gasten to be alone with his wife. "Ellie, our grandson has solved the mystery of how I got hurt. I have no regrets. If this had not happened, we would not have met and I would not have known the love of my life. I miss you and think about you every day. I'm coming home soon." He was wearing his mask again for the first time in over 40 years. Lucy seemed to understand what was happening.

*

Necrotizing fasciitis is caused by numerous types of bacteria from the Streptococcus, Staphylococcus, Clostridium, *and* Vibrio *family where it gets its name "flesh eating". This is an infection of the deep layers of skin and subcutaneous tissues. Although it was first described in 1952, this and other bacterial species such as* Staphylococcus aureus, Clostridium perfringens, *and* Bacteroides fragilis *have been known for years. For example, a* streptococcus *epidemic in 1736 killed some 4000 American colonists. Treatment for bacterial infections involves the use of a combination of antibiotics. Most of these were not known in*

Gasten's day.

Charles knew that the key to determining the cause of Gasten's infection was finding a specific antibody. Normally, a bacterial or viral infection elicits an immune response that protects the host against further infections. In the case of Streptococcus pyogenes, production of IgG antibodies against the M1 protein of the bacterium, facilitates the response to the disease. The M1 protein combines with fibrinogen and IgG to stimulate the migration of neutrophils to the site of formation. A heparin-binding protein is then released from these cells promoting inflammation and cellular necrosis. The absence of an antibody response reduces the virulence of Streptococcus. When the M1 antibody was demonstrated in Gasten's blood, Charles concluded that necrotizing fasciitis was the cause of his disfigurement. What is unknown from this case is whether or not such an antibody can still be produced in Gasten's body some 90 years after the exposure. Many antibodies are produced for life, while others wane over time.

Readers may recognize that this story is a cross between a popular Broadway play and a rather obscure movie entitled, The Legend of 1900. Can someone live on a modern luxury cruise liner undetected for many years then or today? While it might have been possible a century ago, it would be highly unlikely today with the installation of video surveillance throughout the ship.

Antiseptic

I recently attended a small student discussion at the medical center by a senior attending surgeon, Dr. Joseph Murphy. These are informal teaching sessions to a handful of medical students and residents. Dr. Murphy requested that I attend this discussion in case there were any clinical lab-related questions. I was happy to do so because I enjoy interacting with students.

Like many of his contemporaries, myself included, Dr. Murphy was increasingly drawn toward medical history. "You cannot know where you are going until you know where you are," my mentor at Hartford Hospital told me once years ago. On this particular occasion, Dr. Murphy was discussing the medical care of James A. Garfield, the 20th President of the United States. This session was not formal and was without PowerPoint slides. He simply had an open-ended conversation.

"On July 2, 1891, President Garfield was shot twice by Charles Guiteau, who had a minor role in Garfield's election, but was subsequently denied a post in the Garfield Administration. One bullet grazed the President's arm, the other was thought to have lodged somewhere near his liver and spine. A few years earlier, Alexander Graham Bell had invented a metal detector that could have been used to locate the bullet, but they thought the springs on the bed the President was lying on would interfere with the detector signal. So it wasn't used." Dr. Murphy then paused pretending to search for his notes.

"What did they do instead to find the bullet?" one medical student asked as the next logical question.

Dr. Murphy made the previous comment to "set up" the audience for this question. He was a master orator. "The doctors probed inside Garfield's body with their ungloved and unsterilized fingers," Dr. Murphy responded. There were audible gasp among the audience. "You can predict what happened from that moment." Then there was another pause by the surgeon.

"Wait a minute. In the late 1860s, Joseph Lister pioneered antiseptic techniques."

"Shortly thereafter, surgeons at the Royal Glasgow Infirmary were instructed to wear gloves, and wash their hands with 5% carbolic acid solutions," another medical student remarked.

Dr. Murphy replied, "Those practices were not widely used by American surgeons at that time. President Garfield lived for 10 weeks before dying of an infection caused by his doctors. Just before his death, he had lost 100 pounds because his doctors put him on a liquid diet intra-rectally. Apparently, they thought that the bullet was lodged in his intestines. Later at the autopsy, the bullet was found in a non-fatal location in his body. He could have easily survived his wound."

Another medical student grew impatient with the discussion. He wasn't interested in history, just the "here and now." He spoke up. "We obviously would never put dirty hands into a patient today. So what are the current issues facing ICU

24

patients today?"

Dr. Murphy was waiting for this question. It was a lead-in to what he really wanted to discuss with his students on this day. "Bacterial infections continue to be a major cause of morbidity and mortality among patients in an ICU today. Despite our best efforts, healthcare workers are responsible for transmitting infections from one patient to another. There are thousands of cases of "nosocomial infections" each year. If you touch a patient with your gloved or bare hands and don't change the gloves or wash your hands between patients, you are exposing your next patient to these germs. If you use a dirty stethoscope on a patient, this can be a vector for transmission. Although we have known this since the time of Joseph Lister, the situation today is getting worse, not better."

"Why is it getting worse?" a student asked.

"There are several reasons. When I started medicine 30 years ago, ICUs admitted a lot of patients who were basically healthy. They may have needed minor surgery and stayed a day or two for recovery. Today, we do many of these procedures in physician offices as outpatients. Therefore our ICUs now contain a higher proportion of patients who are really sick. These patients are immune compromised." All of the students in the room knew that it was easier for ill patients to catch an infection than someone who has a good immune system.

"What about antimicrobial drug resistance?" the same student asked.

Now we're getting to the meat of the lecture, Dr. Murphy thought. "This is the second major reason why we are seeing more serious infections. I had a patient a few years ago who was in the recovery room following hip replacement surgery....

*

Connie Coswilla worked as an accountant at the city's park district for 35 years. When her husband became ill with cancer, Connie retired from her job to care for him. When he died, she was all alone as they had no children. Connie sold their home and moved into a retirement community. One day when she was 74 years old, Connie slipped when stepping out of the shower and fell onto the hard tiled floor. She heard a crack in her hip and suspected the worse. She had osteoporosis and knew her bones and joints were weak. While lying on the ground, she was able to crawl to the telephone and call for help. When the ambulance arrived, Connie was taken to the hospital. Her family doctor was called and came to the hospital to see his patient. After the examination, he calmly told her that the fall fractured her hip and that she would need it replaced. Connie's facial expression exhibited concern. She was rarely sick and never had surgery before.

"I am going to recommend Dr. Murphy, who is one of our best orthopedic surgeons." These words put Connie's mind at ease. Connie remained in the hospital, and the surgery was scheduled for the day after next. Dr. Murphy and Vincent, a young surgery resident, were in the room discussing her case.

"Mrs. Coswilla, we do dozens of these operations every week," Dr. Murphy told her. "You are otherwise very healthy and we have every expectation for a totally successful procedure." Seeing that Ms. Coswilla was still apprehensive, Vincent spoke to her in hopes of lighting up the mood.

"We are going to put in a new state-of-the art cobalt-chromium-molybdenum alloy joint. We can rebuild you. We have the technology. We can make you better than what you were. Better...stronger... faster." Connie started to laugh. She remembered these lines from the 1970's television show, *The Six Million Dollar Man*. The approach taken by the resident was unconventional. But it worked. It got Connie to relax. She never dreamed that she might become a 'bionic woman.'

The next morning, Connie's hip replacement surgery was conducted and all went well. The broken joint was removed and a metal-on-metal replacement joint was inserted into Connie's left hip. Under general anesthesia, Vincent made the initial incisions and Dr. Murphy performed the joint replacement itself. Cement was added to the tip of her bone to adhere the prosthesis. The surgical procedure took just 90 minutes. Vincent closed the operation by suturing Connie's hip incision. When the operation was over, Connie was wheeled into the recovery room. There were several other patients who were also recovering from a variety of different surgical procedures. After the anesthesia she was given wore off, Vincent visited his patient.

"Now you can run a marathon, Mrs. Coswilla," was his comment.

"I am not ready for that. But I am very grateful to you and Dr. Murphy for fixing me up," Connie said.

Three days after the surgery, she developed a mild fever, 100 degrees. She was scheduled to be transferred to a skilled nursing facility but that was now postponed. Dr. Murphy thought this was a natural reaction to her surgery and that she was not infected. Her medical team took blood and sent it to the microbiology lab for a culture. Knowing that it might take days to get a final report, the team ordered administration of a wide-spectrum antibiotic as a preventative measure. Dr. Murphy had done thousands of hip replacement procedures and wanted to keep her overnight for observation. He was not in favor of antibiotics yet, but he was over-ruled by the ICU team in charge of her care.

"The widespread use of these antibiotics is accelerating the rate of drug resistance for the microorganisms that are present at our hospital," he told them. "We never indiscriminately gave out these drugs to this extent before." But it was to no avail. They told him that medical advice from their malpractice insurance carrier recommended that these patients should be treated prophylactically.

"Are we practicing defensive medicine instead of best practices?" Dr. Murphy asked. Nobody on the team responded. They all knew he was right but could do nothing about it. Dr. Murphy realized that this was the new paradigm. Connie was placed on vancomycin and sent to the ICU.

In retrospect, Connie's ICU team was correct. She had developed an infection due to the presence of enterococci. Unfortunately, the particular strain was resistant to vancomycin. She was put in an isolation ward and treated with other antibiotics. Connie initially developed sepsis, which eventually spread to her nervous system. After a week of hospitalization the infection had spread to her central nervous system and Connie died of meningitis.

"We did this to her," Dr. Murphy said to Vincent, when he found out she passed. "I looked at the medical records of all of the ICU patients on the ward when she was there and all of them were on one antibiotic drug or another. You can't tell me that this was necessary on all of them. Somehow, somebody got sloppy and accidently infected her. Maybe it was poor hand sanitation."

"Maybe it was something she touched," Vincent said.

"Whatever the reason, it was the *environment* that we created causing this." Dr. Murphy had lost patients before, but was visibly disturbed at Connie's death because they promised her there would be no problems. He was particularly upset because the surgery went so well, and it was the events that occurred after that led to her downfall. In that respect, it was not unlike President Garfield after he was shot, but died at the hands of the doctors and nurses trying to help him. Vincent had no words for his mentor. He liked Ms. Coswilla too and turned away before his mentor could see that he was crying.

*

A few months after this case, Dr. Murphy came to the laboratory to ask if we knew of any lab tests that could be used to rule out a bacterial infection in an attempt to minimize the use of wide spectrum antibiotics. Our microbiology lab was just beginning to use molecular techniques that enabled detection of bacteria faster than growing them on a Petrie dish. But these tests are targeted towards specific microorganisms, and it is not possible to test for all microorganisms that can cause an infection. I told him that I would look through the literature to see if such a test existed.

A few months later, I was speaking at a conference in Berlin about cardiac biomarkers. Right after my lecture, the next speaker, Professor Ole Mock, discussed a new laboratory test that was being evaluated at their hospital.

"Procalcitonin is a precursor protein to calcitonin, a calcium regulatory protein," Dr. Mock said. "Patients with a bacterial infection have an increased blood concentration of procalcitonin. The protein is released very early after an infection." Then Dr. Mock said something that really got me interested. "A negative result rules out an infection."

After the lecture, I went up to Dr. Mock and asked, "if the procalcitonin result is negative in an ICU, would this be enough to eliminate use of antibiotics as a precaution?"

"We are exploring a clinical trial to address this very issue. We think that patients who have a negative procalcitonin and are not treated will do just as well or better as those who are treated," Dr. Mock stated. "For patients with an infection, we can continuously monitor procalcitonin concentrations during the course of the patient's hospitalization. When levels begin to drop, this is a sign that the antibiotics are working in eradicating the bacteria. At this point, the patient can be weaned off the drug, perhaps sooner than if we didn't have this test.

"Will these practices stem the tide of bacterial drug resistance?" I asked.

"That is a more difficult question and will require a larger and longer study. But ja, das ist einen hope."

Dr. Mock told me that he was working with a company to make the procalcitonin test, and that it would be available in Europe soon. I went home thinking that we might finally have an answer for Dr. Murphy's question and went to see him. I told him that procalcitonin might be his answer but that he would have to wait until the test was approved and made available in the

U.S. He thanked me and said he looked forward to that day.

The procalcitonin was released in Europe within a year after my visit and it was gradually adopted by European hospitals. I waited for the approval in the U.S. They said it was soon. But after 5 years of waiting, the test was no closer to being available in the U.S. than before. I went to see Dr. Murphy to find out what he knew of the subject.

"Yes, this test has been accepted by my European colleagues, and I believe it has reduced the incidence of wide-spectrum antibiotic use among their patients" Dr. Murphy said. "But we have a problem here in the U.S. that has made it difficult to get our ICU docs interested in the test."

"What could that possibly be?" I asked, thinking that Dr. Murphy and I would be among the first to advocate this test if we had it.

"Don't get me wrong, I think it would be great. But we are fearful of malpractice litigation. If we go against standard medical practice and don't treat someone who is a risk for an infection, and that patient gets an infection, it is likely that we will get sued. This is less of a problem in Europe because there are not as many lawyers practicing there. We also have more limits regarding the amount of money that can be awarded to plaintiffs. Unfortunately in America, we have to practice 'defensive medicine.' which means doing things to 'cover our ass' rather than adopting what might be the best medical practice," Dr. Murphy said. "Until this becomes a standard of practice, it may be a while before we can use this test."

I left the room disgusted. How could this system become so perverse? *We have become a third world country when it comes to some medical practices* I thought.

*

Hip replacement is the most common surgical procedure conducted among the elderly. Arthritis and osteoporosis weaken joints to the point that they need prostheses. New joints can be made of metal, ceramic, or plastic. Artificial joints are not as durable as our human bones, but can last 20 years or more. Over time, metal-on-metal joints leach elemental chromium and cobalt into the circulation which can lead to toxicities termed metallosis. Symptoms include neurologic problems, thyroid disease and heart failure. When this happens, these joints require replacement.

The Centers for Disease Control and Prevention (CDC) estimates that infections contribute to about 100,000 deaths per year. Costs associated with "hospital-acquired infections" are up to $11 billion. Enterococcus is a Gram positive bacterium that are circular in shape and form in pairs or short chains. Prior to the determination of the bacteria's genetic signature, they had an appearance like the Streptococcus species. Enterococcus are naturally resistant to some common antibiotics such as penicillin and cephalosporins but can be eradicated by vancomycin. Enterococcus species that are vancomycin-resistant are particularly virulent. A report from the CDC estimates 20,000 cases of vancomycin resistant Enterococcus occur each year in the US, with about 1,300 deaths. Most infections are hospital-acquired.

Today, the procalcitonin test is widely used in Western European countries. Studies have shown that implementation of the procalcitonin test has led to a reduction in the rate of antibiotic resistance. While there are a few procalcitonin tests that have been approved by the FDA, they are not yet on main-stream chemistry analyzers. This has slowed the adoption of this test in the U.S. by American ICU physicians. Even when it is available, the test has not appeared in clinical practice guidelines and is not used.

Twin Infections

The relationship between identical twins is very special. The lifelong bond between them is unlike those between other siblings or even between fraternal twins. Terry and Tommy Tucker were no exception. They were inseparable growing up. Their friends and teachers had difficulty recognizing one over the other. Their mother solved this problem by buying different clothes for each child, her only children. As they grew older and decided their own wardrobes, Terry preferred collared shirts, tight-fitting pants and white tennis shoes, while Tommy liked tee-shirts, baggy pants, and multi-colored running shoes. Although they have the same genetic makeup, Tommy grew an inch taller and was more athletic than Terry, who was more the intellectual type. After graduation from high school, Tommy attended a college that had a reputation of being a party school on the West Coast. Terry enrolled at an Ivy League School. Despite the geographic distance and time zone difference, Terry and Tommy kept in almost daily contact with each other through phone calls, emails, and social media.

Both boys came home in June after their freshmen year, and they had summer jobs in town. Tommy was a lifeguard and Terry was a tutor. During the Labor Day weekend, just before the boys were scheduled to return to school, they attended a going away party for their parents.

"Your father and I are going to a private island, with no phones, pagers, Internet or email access" their mother told the boys. Her husband and the twin's father was a doctor who was always on call. "I have him all to myself for the next 2 weeks." Both boys were happy for their mother who was always there for their needs, while their father was often at the hospital.

The event was held at the local country club. During the reception, the twins sat with Carmella, a high school friend of theirs. Carmella had just returned from a semester abroad where she worked with underprivileged children in Guangzhou, China. Although all of them were underage, Carmella's older brother was the bartender at the event, and he slipped them alcohol-containing beverages. Nobody at the event seemed to care.

"Try this one, Carm," as the brother gave her the glass.

After taking a sip, she said "This is way too sour for me." He had given his sister a Midori Sour, a combination of honeydew melon liquor, lemon juice and grenadine. She was about to discard it when Tommy, never one to see alcohol go to waste, spoke up.

"Give it here," and he took a big gulp of it. "Wow, this is great. Hey Terry, give this a try."

"Come on, Tommy, you know I don't enjoy drinking." The twins did not enjoy alcohol equally.

"One sip won't kill you," Tommy said.

Terry drank from the glass, made a sour puss face, and put it down.

What Carmella didn't know was that she was in the

incubation phase of an influenza virus she contracted while in China. By sharing the drink, she inadvertently infected both Tommy and Terry. The incubation period for the Asian flu is typically a few days but can be up to 21 days. Both Terry and Tommy became sick within a week of their return to their schools. Their symptoms were the same including fever, cough, sore throat, and muscle weakness. They were first seen at each of their school's infirmary. Like many colleges, this was a clinic which referred more serious illnesses to neighboring hospitals. There were some diagnostic tests available at the infirmary, including a rapid influenza diagnostic test. This assay is like a home pregnancy test. A sample is added and reacts with reagents contained within the device. A line appears on the test pad, if nucleoproteins from the virus are present.

The rapid immunoassay flu test makes use of a nasal pharyngeal swab to collect the sample. A specimen was collected independently on both boys and the testing was conducted. A "Q-tip-" like swab is inserted into the nasal cavity until it reaches resistances. The swab is rotated three times to absorb as much secretion as possible. The swab is removed and placed into a vial containing a preservative. This is what was used for testing.

At the clinic where Terry was, the nurse said to the doctor on duty: "The flu test was negative. Should we send the student back to the dorm?"

The doctor replied, "This is not a surprising result as it is not flu season right now. He probably has a common cold. Give him this script for codeine, Benadryl, and a cough suppressant." By the word "script," the nurse knew that he meant a prescription. "Instruct him to get rest and drink plenty of fluids.

We'll send off the nasopharyngeal swab for a culture but it could take up to a week before we get a result back. I think it will be negative anyway. Who is the next patient?" the doctor asked.

At about the same time, and at the clinic where Tommy was, some 3000 miles away, the nurse said to the doctor on duty: "The flu test was negative. Should we send the student back to the dorm?"

The doctor concluded, "I think this is more than a common cold. Even though it is not flu season, I don't believe the test result is correct. This could be a serious infection. Call for an ambulance and have him transported to the General Hospital. If they think it is nothing, they can send him back to the dorm." The nurse paused, looked at the young doctor like he was being overly cautious, but said nothing and went to the phone to call the ambulance service they usually used. Most students including Tommy didn't have cars so this was the only means for him to get to the hospital. The ambulance arrived within minutes and Tommy was on his way.

At the General Hospital's emergency department, the staff saw that Tommy's body temperature was another degree higher than what was recorded in the clinic. He was breathing fast and his body began to shake. He was admitted into our Intensive Care Unit. The "sepsis" protocol was initiated. This involves a series of steps including ordering specific diagnostic tests such as a blood culture, lactate as a measure of anaerobic metabolism, and measurement of a protein called procalcitonin. In addition, patient isolation procedures were invoked to minimize the spread of infection from patient to patient and from patient to healthcare worker.

The infectious disease service was responsible for Tommy's care. A group of doctors and residents, who were gowned and masked, gathered around his bed later that morning to discuss his case. The head of the team was Dr. Yokoi Kush. Blood and respiratory swabs were collected and sent to the microbiology laboratory for bacterial and viral cultures. A tube was also inserted into Tommy's throat where a "lavage" fluid was squirted into his lungs and then the fluid is aspirated back out of the tube and into a specimen cup. The bronchial lavage specimen was also sent to the lab and cultured for microorganisms. By collecting both a nasal and bronchial sample, he had both the upper and lower respiratory infection covered. Dr. Kush inquired if Tommy had been given a flu vaccine. Tommy said that it was scheduled for the week of his return to school after Labor Day.

The senior resident asked Dr. Kush, "should we initiate wide spectrum antibiotic and anti-viral treatment now while we wait for results of the cultures?" The resident knew from experience that viral cultures in particular could take many days or even weeks to produce a result.

"Normally I would say yes" was Dr. Kush's response. "But the microbiology laboratory has recently implemented a reverse transcription polymerase chain reaction test for viruses and some bacteria. We will have a result later today." Dr. Kush was an expert on drug resistant bacteria. He lectured throughout the U.S. and world on the dangers of overuse of wide spectrum antibiotics. Picking one drug out as an example, he said to the group "Overuse of drugs such as amoxicillin can cause bacteria to mutate such that our current antibiotic drugs will no longer be effective." All of the residents knew that this was a serious medical problem among infectious diseases. "It can also alter Tommy's natural microbiotic flora." These are the bacteria that are found in the skin, mouth, and gastrointestinal tract and perform important metabolic functions for the human host. Amazingly, some scientists have determined that even a healthy person has 10 times more microorganisms than human cells.

"We will make a therapeutic decision later this afternoon when I get the results. These few hours won't affect Tommy's outcome."

*

A few months earlier, I assisted our microbiology laboratory in evaluating and implementing a molecular test for influenza. At the time, my lab had more experience with molecular assays. The most common cause of the flu is infection by the Influenza A or B virus. The test involves extracting nucleic acid from a nasopharyngeal swab, and boosting the sensitivity of the assay by making more copies of the viral RNA using a technique called polymerase chain reaction. This is similar to a photocopy machine that makes replicates of a document. The flu assay we used was able to identify the presence of influenza by detecting their specific RNA sequence. The presence of these nucleic acids in a patient with respiratory tract symptoms indicates infection with the virus. The test that we evaluated was sensitive to both influenza A and B, but not C. Infections by flu C are rare. This latter virus is not as contagious or deadly.

Within a few hours, the assay was reported as positive for the A strain. Dr. Kush was paged and the result was reported. "Just as I suspected" he said to his students when he received the report. Tommy has been infected with influenza. I suspect it is H1N1 or the swine flu. We will start him on a dose of oseltamivir immediately. We need to report this case to the Department of Public Health. They will do an epidemiology investigation.

That same afternoon, Tommy started seizing while in the ICU. He was intubated and placed on medications that sedated him. He was not able to communicate with the Public Health doctors when they came to interview him about his infection. A call was placed to his parents but there was no answer. When they contacted the father's office, they were told that Tommy's parents were on their second honeymoon and no emergency contact information was left. Tommy's father should have known better given that he was a doctor himself. When an email was sent to his home and work address, an automatic response was posted stating that the doctor was unavailable. The group went to Tommy's dormitory to interview his roommates and hall-mates. None of them were experiencing any flu-like symptoms. The cause of the infection could not be determined. Nobody knew about Tommy's exposure to Carmella or her foreign travel. It would be several days before anybody found out that Tommy had a twin brother and that he was suffering from these same symptoms. When he was finally tracked down, they found out that Terry continued to be sick and wasn't hospitalized until two days after the onset of his symptoms. By the time he arrived in the ICU, his infection had gone to the point of no return and he died of his infection. The result of his viral culture was returned to the clinic where he was seen, 3 days after he died. To no one's surprise, the result was positive for influenza A.

Tommy was successfully treated with his anti-viral therapy. However, when he was told that his brother had the same infection but died of this illness, he went into a deep depression. Tommy was moved from the intensive care unit to a private bed. He just sat in his bed looking at the ceiling thinking about the life he had with his brother. He cried himself to sleep every night. He didn't have an appetite and lost 25 pounds to his already slim figure. He questioned why he survived and his brother didn't. Shortly thereafter, his parents finally returned from their honeymoon and did their best to console their only surviving son. They too felt guilty about not being available during the critical time of their medical emergencies. Tommy was seen by a psychiatrist who treated him with a mild antidepressant. Eventually he was weaned off the drug, and was able to return to school in the second semester.

*

According to the World Health Organization, the worldwide death toll for the 2009 swine flu pandemic was nearly 300,000 people. Most of the deaths occurred in Southeast Asia and Africa. The major causes of death were respiratory and cardiovascular diseases. In the U.S., there were some 50 million infections with about 10,000 deaths, mostly among children and young adults. There are three influenza viruses, named "A", "B", and "C". Influenza "A" is the one most commonly encountered in the U.S. There are several subtypes of flu A, based on surface proteins on the virus itself. The hemagglutinin protein or "H" enables the virus to attach to cells of the upper respiratory tract and to hemoglobin. The protein is so named because binding to red cells causes these cells to aggregate. There are currently 18 different hemagglutinin subtypes. The neuraminidase protein or "N" is an enzyme that enables the virus to replicate within the host. There are 11 different subtypes to this protein. The influenza subtype responsible for the Swine flu pandemic of 2009 was termed "The H1N1."

Vaccines to influenza are readily available. Each season, the CDC analyzes prevalence data and recommends which stains should be included in a seasonal vaccine. The flu season for the Northern Hemisphere is the opposite of that in the Southern Hemisphere and different vaccines are used. The elderly and health care workers are especially vulnerable and getting vaccinated is highly recommended. Due to the rarity of a flu C infection, vaccines do not usually protect against this virus.

I was lecturing in China during the 2009 swine flu pandemic and was traveling with my son. At the Beijing airport, there were thermal imaging cameras that were aimed at arriving passengers looking for those with increased body temperatures. Individuals thought to be infected were quarantined for days and weeks at a time. Luckily my son and I were not infected. We did not have a fever, so we were allowed entry. We were amazed to see so many Chinese citizens wearing facial masks to protect themselves from infected individuals. H1N1 is transmitted through the air.

The molecular test for influenza enables a much more rapid diagnosis of infection than a viral culture. This can have a significant impact on treatment of patients suspected of disease, as in Tommy's case. The test is not yet available in the majority of hospitals and medical centers. New diagnostic tests must undergo a long, time consuming verification step to fully understand the attributes of the test and how it might improve clinical outcomes. The test itself is also much more expensive than the rapid immunoassay.

The U.S. Centers for Disease Control and Prevention has

recommended that patients with symptoms of a flu infection be treated with antiviral medications even before the causative agent has been identified. In Terry's case, the failure to recognize and treat influenza during the initial stages of the infection led to the boy's unfortunate death.

A person who has a twin brother or sister who has died is termed a "twinless twin." Many have described themselves as having lost half of themselves. The depression that follows is a complication well-recognized among psychiatrists. Twinless twins can find some solace within support groups of others who have lost a fraternal or identical twin. There have been celebrities who survived the death of a twin. Elvis Presley had a brother, Jesse, who was stillborn. When Elvis was young, he received counselling from Liberace, who was another twinless twin.

Mysophobia

She started out as a comedienne. She was a regular at the *Standup*, a comedy night club in Manhattan Beach and performed to a small audience of about 50 people on Friday nights along with other Hollywood wannabes. Jason Allen was also a regular at the club and appeared on Saturday nights. He was not available during the week, as he was busy in Culver City filming of *After Hours Show with Jason Allen*. The club's manager, Jason's long-time friend, told him about Connie and showed Jason some video footage of her act. She joked that she was single because she was afraid of direct physical contact with humans.

"I never shake hands with anyone who I meet for the first time," she said during one of her gigs. "Especially Men. Men are disgusting. I've seen how my older brothers behave. They gorge themselves with spicy foods and then take turns trying to out burp and out fart each other. My brother would extend his hand and when you shook it, there would be this prolonged audible leakage of noxious vapor. It takes talent to regulate your anal sphincter like a high pressure methane gas regulator. Then when it was time to go to the bathroom, they would sit there for 15 minutes or more, reading car racing magazines the whole while. So naturally when I meet strange men for the first time, I can only think back to when I was a kid. '*Where has THAT hand been?*' I would ask myself." This always garnered a laugh and sort of became her trademark line. It was these childhood memories that caused Connie to have mysophobia, a fear of germs. Jason was amused but bathroom humor was never his style. Fortunately, Connie commented on other differences between men and women and she had a nice comedic delivery.

At Jason's request, the club manager invited Connie to be an opening act for Jason during one of his Saturday *Standup* shows. She received lots of laughs from the crowd and it got them in a good mood for Jason's monologue. At the end of the night, Connie was summoned to meet Jason in his dressing room. When he extended his hand, Connie raised both her hands up, palms out, and did not grab Jason's hand to shake it.

"So this is real? You really are a germaphobe?" he asked her.

"Yeah, I have been all my life. But this interferes with my social life," she told him.

Her attitude towards physical contact was just the opposite of Jason's. At the beginning of his shows, he shook hands and "high fived" dozens of the people from the studio audience who came to see him. This rapport served him well during his entire *After Hours Show* run of 15 years. After a few minutes of talk in his dressing room, Jason told her that he was going to give her a guest shot on television. Through his show, Jason had launched the careers of many comedians, just like Johnny Carson did decades before him. Naturally, Connie was thrilled. She jumped up and was about to hug him, but then composed herself. *Where has HE been?* was her germaphobic thought. She gave him her contact information and Jason left the nightclub and his driver took him home.

Connie appeared on Jason's show a few months later. The television studio audience loved her. Instead of a music number that night, Connie's bit was the closing act of the show. There wasn't time for her to be an actual guest and sit with Jason while on the air. Since she lived in the Los Angeles area, the *After Hours Show* producers would sometimes call her to substitute for a guest who cancelled at the last minute and she became somewhat of a regular guest host. While she was never the head-lining guest, she did get to sit in the guest chair to the left of Jason and the audience came to know her a little better. Connie had an engaging personality and Jason never had to worry about filling up time with her like he sometimes had to do with some of the celebrities that were booked. He genuinely liked her and was happy to have her on the show from time to time.

The studios took notice of how comfortable she was in front of a camera. A few years later a producer asked her to audition to be a host of a new daytime game show called *Family Fights*. She made the short list of candidates, all but her were men. She was told that it was a show where families compete against other families with a series of questions and perform physical tasks. During the introduction, Connie was asked to introduce the families and question them about their lives. Connie was brilliant during a practice run of the show and she was pegged to be the new show's host. The show was mildly popular on the game show network, but never made it to any of the major networks or on prime time. It was only after she was offered the job that she told them that she had mysophobia. The producers agreed that the host did not have any physical contact with contestants, and that the studio would keep multiple containers of hand sanitizers on the set.

*

Connie's only outlet from work was playing soccer. She was a goalie on a club team in Pasadena where she lived. She had played throughout high school and was the goalie. This position did not require much physical contact with her sweaty teammates or any of the players which suited her well. She told her teammates from the very beginning that giving "high-fives" was not her thing. They competed against other teams in the area. One of the games was played on artificial turf. She had never played on such a surface before and was amazed at how fast the ball moved. During one play, she dove to her left to successfully block a shot. Her team won the game that day, but when she returned home, she noticed that her right knee had a nasty scrape as the result of the shot she saved. She put antiseptic ointment on it, covered the wound with a bandage and didn't think anything further about it.

Within a few days, however, the wound on her knee did not heal and instead became infected. She put on more neosporin. Soon, other lesions began to appear on other parts of her body including her face. At first, she was able to cover up the outbreak with makeup. But when it did not get better, the show's producers were forced to put her show on temporary hiatus. They told her to see a doctor.

Connie arrived at the General on a Thursday. She was immediately placed into the ICU ward under isolation. Nobody was allowed in her room unless they wore special sterile gowns, gloves, and masks. There was a sink outside her door and everyone exiting the room had to wash their hands.

Sputum and blood samples were sent to the laboratory for cultures. At the time, we did not offer a molecular test for the causative agent. So it took several days before the identity of the bacterial agent could be made. In the meantime, Connie was treated with a wide spectrum antibiotic. Eventually, she was diagnosed with *Staphylococcus aureus*. It was later determined that this particular strain of bacteria was resistant to beta lactam-type antibiotics such as penicillin and methicillin. It was termed MRSA, or methicillin-resistant *Staph aureus*.

*

As part of our training program to laboratory medical technology students and postdoctoral fellows, we go on lab medicine "rounds" whereby we regularly visit patient wards and discuss relevant clinical laboratory tests results. Most clinical laboratorians spend their entire day in the lab and never see how their results are actually being used to make medical decisions. These sessions are hosted by our pathology residents who review case histories and provide a summary of clinical laboratory test findings to the group. On one day in particular, the resident selected Connie's case. When I found out that we were discussing a public figure, I warned my staff that disclosure of a patient's medical information to anyone who is not part of the patient's healthcare team was prohibited and can result in significant fines and criminal charges to those who violate patient privacy. We were justified in attending because we provide laboratory results that are part of patient care. With this preface, my resident proceeded cautiously to present her case. We did not gown up and enter her isolated room. As such, she could not hear what was being said and was asleep in her bed. But through the observation window, we could clearly see extensive pus-filled lesions throughout her face, arms, and legs. These parts of her skin were not covered because blankets would have caused skin irritation. To me, her appearance was dramatically different from what she looked like on television. She was hardly recognizable.

The resident described the laboratory procedure that was conducted in order to diagnose this infection. "Under the microscope, Staphylococcus, as the name implies, are round, globe-shaped organisms that turn blue with the application of the Gram stain. We then grew colonies from a sputum sample using an appropriate media. Biochemical tests from colonies taken from the culture are performed to determine that this is *Staphlycoccus aureus* and not some other coccal bacteria."

"How did she contract this?" one of my students asked.

My laboratory medicine resident responded, "From the medical record, it appears to have started from an abrasion suffered playing soccer on a field that contained an artificial turf. There have been many cases of MRSA infection amongst athletes, although in most cases, it was infections spread in the locker room by sharing towels or not sanitizing whirlpools."

While we were standing there, several other doctors were leaving her room and removing their personal protective equipment. Each of them thoroughly washed their hands. While they were doing that, I started singing the "*Happy Birthday*" song quietly, but loud enough so that my students could hear me but the doctors near the sink couldn't. One of the newer students, Fay, looked at me and I could tell that she thought I was off my rocker. But most of the other students knew what I was doing. I explained to Fay that the proper duration for hand washing is the same amount of time needed to sing this song.

"I tell all my students to do this which serves as a reminder to not short cut this important infection control step," I told her.

While my resident continued on with his discussion, Fay was watching the next doctor who went to wash his hands. I could tell that she was singing this song in her mind, and each of the doctors had cleansed themselves properly. I didn't mind that I had distracted some of my students away from the discussion at hand. *This lesson for Fay was far more important than the details of Connie's case,* I thought to myself.

"They all did it long enough. It works!" she said to me off to the side.

Learning from my resident that Connie suffered from mysophobia, I said to Fay, "Our patient would have approved of the hand washing practices performed by her doctors."

*

Connie had a severe case of MRSA and spent the next month in the hospital. Her lifestyle of repeated hand washing made her susceptible to an infection because it removed her resident skin flora, making it easier for the opportunistic MRSA strain to invade. Connie suffered scars from the infection on her body and face. Her show was cancelled. Because of her altered appearance, she was not given any new opportunities in Hollywood. This is a tough town which cherishes beauty. While Connie was never gorgeous, the producers did not want anyone on camera with a liability in their appearance.

An infectious disease specialist told Connie that her excessive hand sanitation practices contributed to her contracting a MRSA infection. She was lucky that her infection did not affect her organs such as her heart. Connie was told to see a psychiatrist to treat her affliction. Wanting to be more normal, she complied. She was diagnosed with "blood-infection-injury phobia" and obsessive compulsive disorder. She was treated by a technique known as "cognitive behavior therapy." A female therapist created exercises to help her over her affliction. The therapist would thoroughly wash her hands in front of Connie to show that she was clean. Then she told Connie to massage the therapist's hands including the cracks between all of her fingers on both hands. Connie cognitively knew there were no germs, but she had never touched someone's hands in this way before. In later sessions, the exercise would be repeated except the therapist would wash her hands out of Connie's direct view. Later still, a man came and performed the exercise. Eventually, there was no hand washing in her presence, and she was told to trust them.

These counseling sessions were effective and her mysophobia abated considerably. Connie left the Los Angeles area and moved to Texas where she married and became a mom shortly thereafter. Later she became a soccer coach when her children grew older. None of her children suffered from a fear of germs. Connie went back into television.

*

A few weeks after we attended rounds on Connie, I was summoned to appear in front of one of our privacy officers. These individuals regularly monitor who has access to private medical records and it was noticed that one of my residents had electronically accessed her file. Since Connie was a celebrity she was put on a special list, and I had to justify why it was necessary. I told them that Connie's MRSA infection was unusual in terms of how severe it was and how she contracted it. The privacy officer knew that most hospital cases were spread from contact with healthcare workers. "This was not the case here, but we used this as an example of the importance sanitation to avoid hospital-acquired infections." As we are a university hospital, this was an acceptable justification for our file review. But then I received the standard privacy warning regarding future encounters. *Celebrities are no different from other patients*, I thought to myself as I was leaving his office.

*

Staphylococcus aureus is a common gram positive bacterium that is found in the skin and the anterior nares of the nose. It is part of resident flora and produces no harm. For some individuals, however, a Staph infection can cause skin infections manifested by pimples, boils, and abscesses. These bacteria exert their pathologic damage by releasing chemicals that are toxic to human cells.

Through bacterial resistance, nature has created a pathway that enables some of the bacteria to escape destruction by man-made drugs. Over the years, these microorganisms have mutated in such a way that penicillin-like drugs are no longer effective. Infections by methicillin-resistant Staphylococcus aureus can cause significant illnesses if not treated early and effectively. Fortunately, there are next-generation antibiotics that are effective against MRSA. Many states including California require reporting of hospital-acquired MRSA, estimated to be about 85% of all cases, with appropriate isolation of patients who are colonized.

Connie was not the only game show host who was afraid of direct human contact.   Deal or No Deal's Howie Mandel's germaphobic aversion is well chronicled in his autobiography, Here's the Deal: Don't Touch Me. *There he described a chronic obsessive disorder that caused him to wash his hands repeatedly and use hand sanitizers when a sink was not readily available. As a child, he never re-tied his shoe laces when they came undone because of the laces' exposure to the ground. In hotels, he would carry an ultraviolet light in an attempt to eliminate bacteria. He admits that his removal of germs on his body has probably made him more prone to infections than normal. This may have occurred with Connie as well.*

Transmission of MRSA through exposure from artificial turf has been described previously. Materials used to produce these playing surfaces are known to retain the viability of bacteria which promotes infection of unsuspecting athletes. Several members of the Tampa Bay Buccaneers professional football team have been infected with MRSA, thought to have occurred through open wounds created by the abrasive surface of fake grass. Sanitizing artificial turf is not yet regularly performed. Fortunately, these fields are slowly being replaced by natural turf because they are softer and are associated with fewer injuries.

It was ironic that Connie was always fearful of an infection from human contact. Despite her precautions, she unknowingly became infected by another female goalie who was on the field before her, and left some of her body fluids on the playing field.

Not This or That

An anonymous person once asked, "Why do bad things happen to good people?" This question is relevant when speaking about Martha Anderson. Here was a woman who was kind, and well-liked by everyone she met, but had a series of medical mishaps that would plague her for her entire life.

It all began in 1982 when Martha was in college. She was the number one player on her school's tennis team. She learned how to play at the age of 4 years from her father, Richard, who was a high school boy's tennis coach. Richard taught her how to hit a two-handed backhand because she wasn't strong enough to swing the racket with one hand. By the time she was 8 her father entered her into local tournaments. Within 3 years, she was winning junior tournaments, beating both girls and boys who were a few years older than she. While she could have played professionally, she decided to play college tennis first.

Martha's medical problems began on the day when the school had a match against the rival State University. She was traveling on the team bus when the driver with the entire team onboard was entering the highway at a fast rate of speed. The bus did not make the merge quick enough and the bus hit the guard rail head on. None of the seats had belts, as they weren't used or required back then. Martha was standing in the aisle talking to her coach when the accident occurred. The girls and coaches were thrown about the bus. Many of them were taken to the local hospital. Martha received the worse of it. She flew forward into the bus' windshield, suffering a concussion and a broken right shoulder blade, and she was bleeding internally. She underwent emergency surgery to repair her shoulder and to stop the bleeding. The surgery took 5 hours. The surgeons called our lab and we mobilized the "massive transfusion" protocol anticipating that there would be many units of blood necessary to stop her internal bleeding and replace the blood she lost. All of these units that Martha received were from anonymous donors.....

*

John Joseph suffered from depression off and on for his entire life. He would have bouts that would last for weeks making it difficult for him to focus and maintain steady employment. When he lost his last job, he was evicted from his low-rent apartment and became homeless. It wasn't too long thereafter that John began abusing cocaine and heroin. Sharing needles was a common practice in the area where he lived. In order to feed his addiction, John did whatever he could to make money. This included pan handling to people in the neighborhood, recycling discarded bottles and aluminum cans for their deposits, and donating his blood and sperm at the University. John knew that the blood bank and sperm bank would not accept him as a donor if they knew he was homeless. So in order to be presentable, he would shower and shave on the day of the scheduled donation, and put on clean clothes he received from the shelter. When registering, he gave the bank's staff a fake address and denied any recreational drug use.

During the 1980s, the blood bank tested donated blood for the presence of antibodies to hepatitis A and B. While it was known that other forms of hepatitis existed and caused liver damage, the virus responsible for these infections had not yet been identified and there was no test for its presence. Instead, our blood bank lab tested donor blood for a liver enzyme called "alanine aminotransferase" or ALT. High levels of this enzyme in the blood suggested that the donor might be infected and these units were discarded. While this offered some protection against the transfusion of tainted blood, this "surrogate test" was not perfect. Infected individuals can harbor the virus in their blood without any symptoms of liver disease for many weeks, months and even years, and transmit the disease to others. One day on his way to the blood bank at the University Hospital, he stopped to watch the women's tennis team, who was practicing on their courts nearby, getting ready for their match against the State University. Martha was working on hitting overheads with her coach. Martha hit one practice shot so hard that when it hit the court, it bounced over the fence. The ball landed near Joseph, who picked it up and threw it back onto the court. Martha saw what he had done and thanked him before returning to her practice session.

*

Pins and plates were inserted into Martha's shoulder to help repair her damaged tendons and bones. She feared her competitive tennis days were over. Her recovery would require a week in the hospital and a month of rehab. Her doctor told her that her shoulder injury would greatly affect her tennis game, particularly her serve and overhead. Martha knew that she could no longer play at a high level. She voluntarily gave up her athletic scholarship from the University to another deserving girl.

About two months after her injury, Martha developed malaise, anorexia, and weakness. She went to see Dr. Julius Stone, their family doctor. Dr. Stone reviewed Martha's surgical record and saw that she had been subjected to several blood transfusions during her operation. He had a notion as to what was happening, and ordered a battery of laboratory tests to confirm his suspicion. When the lab tests came back, he sat down with Martha and her father Richard to review the findings.

"You have an increased level of ALT and other liver enzymes," he said while looking at the report. "Your serum bilirubin concentration, which is a sign of liver obstruction, is also increased."

"What does this mean?" Richard asked.

"I think you have contracted hepatitis," Dr. Stone said.

Richard had some knowledge of the disease and asked, "is it hepatitis A or hepatitis B?" He was hoping for the "A" strain, as infection by this virus is mild, self-limiting, and rarely fatal. Hepatitis B can be very dangerous. Dr. Stone's answer puzzled Richard.

"It is not this or that," was his response.

"Are you trying to be funny?" Richard said, annoyed at what appeared to be a flippant response.

"What I meant to say is that we know what it isn't. Her tests were negative for hepatitis A and B, yet we know that it is hepatitis. But we cannot identify the exact virus," Dr. Stone said.

Richard was confused more than ever but before he

could pose another question, Dr. Stone continued. "Your daughter has a disease called 'non-A, non-B hepatitis." Dr. Stone went on to explain that this was a relatively new viral infection. "We don't have any drugs to treat this form of hepatitis. At this time, we can only hope that the virus will go away on its own."

But that didn't happen. Martha developed a chronic hepatitis infection. In 1989, scientists discovered and isolated the virus that was responsible for the vast majority of non-A, non-B hepatitis cases, and the virus was named "hepatitis C." Martha's blood was re-tested a few years later and it was confirmed to be hepatitis C. But knowing the causative agent didn't help Martha's condition. The virus continued to eat away at her liver. It would be many years before dual therapy based on pegylated interferon alfa and ribavirin would be available. Ten years after her initial blood transfusion, Martha's liver disease progressed to the next phase. Dr. Stone sent Martha to see a liver specialist. Under local anesthesia, the hepatologist inserted a long needle through her abdomen and removed a small piece of her liver. The biopsy was sent to the pathology laboratory. After carefully examining the tissue under a microscope, the surgical pathologist wrote in his report of the presence of mononuclear inflammation, fibrosis that bridged between her portal veins, and she had significant liver necrosis. Martha, at the age of 30, had hepatic cirrhosis. When Dr. Stone saw this report, it came as somewhat of a surprise. Martha was not a drinker or drug user, and she did not have any other comorbid conditions such diabetes, or a co-infection with hepatitis B or human immunodeficiency virus which had been recently discovered.

A few years later, Martha's disease progressed to the last

stage. She had hepatocellular carcinoma. While this form of cancer is common among Asians, the frequency among Americans is relatively low. Blood tests showed a high concentration of a tumor marker known as alpha-fetoprotein, a test that we offer in my laboratory. She was treated with chemotherapy but it failed to arrest her tumor growth. Liver transplantation surgery was just beginning in the early 1990s and was not available to Martha. A repeat liver biopsy and CT scan revealed that her disease was metastatic and the cancer had spread to other organs. Surgical removal of the tumor would not be effective since the tumor had spread to her other organs. There was nothing her oncologist could do. Martha died of liver cirrhosis and cancer a year later at the age of 33.

*

Dr. Stone was greatly upset at Martha's death. Sure, all doctors lose patients, but Martha was special and Dr. Stone admired her strength and determination. Throughout her disease, Martha remained upbeat and optimistic. She never questioned why she contracted this disease or blamed anyone for it. During her last days with her family surrounding her, she thanked them and the Lord for their love and support and she was at peace when she died.

*

A dozen years later, Dr. Stone retired from his practice. He was clearing out his inactive medical records of his patients and ran across Martha's file. The epidemiology of hepatitis C infection was now well known, so he took out his notes and compared Martha's case against the literature. While chronic hepatitis C occurs in about 75% of acute infections, the incidence of chronicity is lower for patients under 25 years. Men had a higher rate of chronic hepatitis C than women, and African American and Asian populations are at higher risk than Caucasians such as Martha. Even Martha's increased serum bilirubin level, measured at the time of her acute infection went against the typical course. Patients with jaundice, an indicator of high bilirubin, have a higher rate of virological clearance. Martha's infection resulted in chronic disease and she died from it.

*

Across town, John Joseph continued to live his life without social values. He recovered from his hepatitis C infection, which did not develop into a chronic disease. He did contract an HIV infection from his continued intravenous drug use, and he was lucky that it occurred after anti-retroviral therapy became available. His AIDS was successfully treated. Once the blood bank began antibody screening the blood supply for both hepatitis C and HIV, John who was positive for both diseases, was no longer allowed to donate blood. John did infect many women through unprotected sex. The sperm bank also stopped accepting donations from him, but by that time, his semen was used to impregnate several women whose husbands were infertile or impotent. He was an anonymous father to many children. Today, John continues to live on the street begging for money and using it to buy drugs.

In response to the opening question of why bad things happen to good people, a rather unsatisfying answer is, "to balance out the good things that happen to bad people."

*

Approximately 3% of the global population of the world is infected with hepatitis C. Unlike hepatitis B, there are no vaccines for hepatitis C, largely because the virus mutates rapidly. The incidence of hepatitis C infection has declined dramatically in the U.S. since blood banks instituted testing for the virus in 1992. The increasing use of condoms during intercourse and the availability of needle exchange programs for intravenous drug addicts have also contributed to fewer infections. Today, most individuals who are infected with hepatitis C are the baby boomers, born between 1945 and 1965.

There have been many breakthroughs in the diagnosis and management of hepatitis C, none of which was available in Martha's time. There are 6 known genotypes and over 50 subtypes of the virus. Molecular tests are used to determine the virus' genotype. Treatment decisions are partially based on the genotype of the virus. Laboratory diagnosis begins with detecting the anti-hepatitis C antibody. Samples that are positive can be tested with the hepatitis C viral load test. This is an assay that measures the number of hepatitis viral particles detected in blood. The viral load result is useful to confirm the diagnosis, assess how infectious an individual might be, and as a measure of therapeutic response.

Treatment with interferon alfa and ribavirin can produce clearance of the virus and has been the mainstay for treating hepatitis C infection for the last several years. The majority of hepatitis C patients are treated with this drug combination. Recently, a genetic test has become available to predict the success of dual therapy. Doctors can predict who will most likely benefit from dual therapy and who will require a more aggressive regimen. For those who fail drug therapy, liver transplantation is an option. Based on the observation that Martha's disease took its course to the final endpoint it is likely that she had the *genotype that would have required the most aggressive of therapies.*

Within the past few years, antiviral drugs have been approved by the US Food and Drug Administration. These new therapies are very costly, roughly $80,000 per patient treated. These drugs used alone or combined with interferon and ribavirin form a "triple therapy" and they are more effective for treating hepatitis C infections, but are more expensive and patients can suffer more deleterious side effects. For individuals with advanced disease, liver transplantation is the last resort. A hepatitis C infection is the leading reason for liver transplantation today, but it was not an option for Martha back in the early 1990s. These operations were not as widely available or as successful as kidney transplants.

There are dozens of celebrities who have disclosed their infection with hepatitis C, in an effort to gather more public awareness and raise money for research. These include actors Pamela Anderson, Jim Nabors and Ken Watanabe, and singers Gregg Allman, Natalie Cole, and Naomi Judd. Mickey Mantle of the New York Yankees and Ken Kesey, who authored One Flew Over the Cuckoo's Nest, *both died of liver cancer caused by a hepatitis C infection.*

The Kiss of Death

****

It was almost dark. She flew around neighborhood looking for her next meal where she spotted a squirrel. He had just entered his nice and cozy den in a hollowed out tree. *I am going to skip humans for a while.* The last time she was hungry, she tried to a bite girl. But the teenager caught the bug in the act and almost kill the kissing bug with a slap of her hand. *Even after she missed, she kept after me trying to catch me as I tried to fly away.* The squirrel had no defense, and bug landed inside the ear and drew blood from the critter.

*

    Hugo Cruz wanted to make a difference. He came from a middle class family living in a small town in South Central Texas. He received a scholarship to attend the University of Texas in Austin where he majored in social services. When he earned his Bachelor's degree, Hugo took a job at a shelter back home. But before he started employment, he volunteered for Global Housing Inc., a charitable organization that sends volunteers to rural areas of under developed countries to help build housing. Global sent Hugo and other Americans to remote rural locations in South America. For the next three months, Hugo lived in a dormitory with the other volunteers in the village where they were assigned. Overall, it was a very rewarding experience. Having come from a small town himself, he could relate to many of the residents living there. Hugo understood how difficult it was for the families to meet their everyday needs for food, clean water, basic medical care, and shelter. He saw that there were many families living in one small house, all sharing a single bathroom. These dwellings were not actually houses, but more like huts with adobe-like thatched roofs and porous walls. Hugo befriended one woman who had an inquisitive 7-year old boy named Paolo. The boy followed Hugo around asking him questions everywhere they went. Hugo was fluent in Spanish so communication was not a problem. One day, Paolo asked his mother if Hugo could come to their home for dinner one night. She agreed and went to the construction site with her son to invite Hugo.

"We can't offer you anything fancy," Paolo's mother said, "but we want to show our appreciation for what you and your group are doing for us."

"I would love to come," Hugo said. That night, Hugo arrived at 7 pm where he was introduced to some of the other families living in Paolo's home. He thoroughly enjoyed the meal and the company of his new friends. Afterward, he sat on a log outside with Paolo, his mother, and some of the other young children who lived in the house. Hugo had a travel-size guitar that he brought from home and so they started to play and sing for the children. They all knew the American folk songs he played and started singing along. When it was time for Hugo to return to his dorm. Paolo pleaded with Hugo to spend the night with them. There was a spare bed because someone from another family was away that evening. He agreed and he slept in a bed next to Paolo and his mother.

*

As I am the director of the clinical chemistry laboratory at the General, it is important for me to keep abreast of the practices in the other sections of the department including microbiology, hematology, and the blood bank. There was a special presentation headed by Dr. Barry Holden, chief of the microbiology laboratory. There were also members of the hospital infectious disease faculty. The date was December, 2006.

"The FDA has approved the first laboratory test for detecting antibodies in the blood of individuals infected with *Trypanosoma cruzi*, the causative agent in Chagas disease," Dr. Holden stated.

Dr. Arlene Sedor was head of the laboratory's blood bank and responded. "At last, we have been waiting for this test for several years now. There is medical evidence that patients can acquire Chagas disease through the transfusion of infected blood. There has been discussion among blood bankers about screening the blood supply for evidence of this parasitic infection. Now that the test is approved, we can begin to test donated blood."

Normally, I am not that interested in infections that are endemic in other parts of the world but not in the United States. Chagas disease, however, produces cardiac complications which aligns with my research on cardiac biomarkers. So when one of the residents asked about the epidemiology, signs and symptoms, and medical complications of Chagas disease, I was able to contribute to the conversation.

Dr. Holden began the discussion. "There are multiple

routes of transmission including bites of infected insects, oral transmission of infected food, in utero transmission from mother to fetus, and through exposure of contaminated blood. The triatomine or the "kissing bug" is responsible for infections of humans and other mammals. These insects are so named because they like to bite mucous membranes such as the lips and around the eyes. After ingesting the hosts' blood, the bug defecates at the site of the bite, thereby transmitting the parasite. Kissing bugs are nocturnal. A particularly disgusting source of entry is when these insects accidently drop their feces directly into the mouth of a sleeping victim."

"That's one great reason to keep your mouth shut when you sleep," I said to my neighbor seated next to me. Dr. Holden overheard my comment. "You can't always control that, especially if you have sleep apnea."

An infectious disease doctor then spoke. "Shortly after a bite, the victim can experience swelling near the site that can persist for several days or weeks. This can be accompanied by fever, muscle aches, rash, and fatigue. For most people, these symptoms resolve spontaneously and there are no long term medical problems. For a few, particularly those who have weakened immune systems, a chronic phase occurs."

"The two organs that are most effected are the heart and gastrointestinal tract," I stated. "Digestive problems include swallowing difficulties, malabsorption, and weight loss. In many of these patients, there is progression to cardiomyopathy." Everyone in the room knew that this meant heart failure. "This is the leading cause of death in Chagas infected patients. We have serum biomarkers such as BNP that can be used to diagnose this complication."

Then Dr. Sedor spoke up. "By screening the supply of blood from our bank for Chagas disease antibodies, we hope to reduce the mortality of Chagas disease."

*

Hugo was asleep in the hut when the kissing bugs awoke from their slumber and began circulating around the room looking for their evening meal. During the day, triatominae or kissing bugs inhabit roofs made of wood and mud-faced walls. One bug in particular was eyeing Hugo and Paolo. *Let's see, who is going to provide me food today?* The kissing bug hovered over the boy first. *How about this kid?* He quietly landed near his mouth and extended his proboscis, his needle-like nose that would be the conduit for Paolo's blood. Just before penetration, Paolo turned his head aside. The insect quickly pulled away and took flight. *I'll have to select another person.* Hugo was lying on his back with a sheet covering his mid-section, with his head and feet exposed. The bug decided to go after the young man. She swooped down and landed near Hugo's left eye. Hugo was snoring and was sound asleep. The carbon dioxide that Hugo was exhaling was particularly attractive to the insect. When she landed, Hugo did not flinch. The bug first spit out some saliva for lubrication. It also has anticoagulant properties to prevent Hugo's blood from clotting when it is being withdrawn by the insect. The kissing bug then extended her lance piercing his skin and aspirated blood from a capillary surrounding Hugo's eye socket. *Aahhh! Good! This adult male human was indeed an excellent choice.* Hugo had good capillaries blood flow from a strong systolic pulse. The amount of blood quickly filled the bug's abdomen. *Maybe I will stick around for a moment and enjoy the aroma.* She was referring to the CO_2. In order to make more room for the blood, it was natural for her to drop some of her stored poop directly onto Hugo's skin. Afterwards, she slowly flew away feeling completely satiated. She could not fly quickly because of the added weight of Hugo's blood. When she left, she returned to the thatched roof of the room. After landing she though, *I think I am going to take a nap now.* The kissing bug would need a few days to process Hugo's blood before she would need to eat again. First she would first lay some eggs before searching out for her next meal.

The area on Huro where the kissing bug struck produced an itching sensation, which led Hugo to scratch the area with the fingertips of his left hand. This enabled the contaminated feces to enter into this blood through the small wound created by the insect when it was withdrawing Hugo's blood. This particular kissing bug was carrying the *Trypanosoma cruzi* parasite, having contracted it from a squirrel. Hugo was unknowingly infected when he rubbed the bug's feces into his face. Over the next few days, the parasite began to multiply within Hugo's blood.

That morning, Hugo awoke at dawn and prepared to leave the hut. All of the others were still asleep. When Hugo arose, Paolo opened his eyes. Hugo smiled and waved goodbye to his friend. Hugo went back to his dormitory where he showered, dressed in clean clothes, and started his day. Although Hugo was now infected by the protozoan parasite, he did not develop symptoms and never learned of his infection. He had some inflammation around his left eye where the kissing bug struck, but he didn't think anything about it. Working on houses, there

70

would often be bumps and bruises. *Maybe I bumped into a dry wall and didn't know it or remember,* he thought. The swelling resolved after a day, and a few weeks later, he finished his work with Global Housing, and returned to his hometown in Texas to begin his new job. His friends and family noticed that Hugo was more mature now, and was ready to take on the next phase of his life.

Later that month, a convict escaped from the prison in a neighboring town. An all-points bulletin was issued by the local police. A lone officer found the prisoner walking along the road. There was a confrontation. The prisoner was able to wrestle the officer's weapon free shooting him in the abdomen. The convict fled leaving the officer down and bleeding on the roadside. Soon, a passing motorist stopped and immediately called for assistance. The officer was taken to nearby hospital for surgery to repair his wound. Word got out in this small community that the policeman lost a lot of blood and there was a need for blood donors. Hugo, knowing that he was type O, the universal donor, immediately left his office and went to the hospital to donate a pint. The blood was processed and sent to the operating room. But the procedure was nearly completed and no additional blood was needed. Hugo's unused unit was sent to the blood bank for storage.

*

A few weeks after the lecture, I went to see Dr. Sedor still thinking about Chagas' disease. "Don't we keep small amounts of blood that have been transfused into patients for investigation of post-transfusion reactions?" I asked. "Now that we have a blood test, it would be interesting to go back and test some donor blood to see if we transfused units that we now know are positive."

"That's very perceptive," Dr. Sedor said. "We have already done that study. The rate of positivity is under 0.01%. But given the large number of donations nationwide, there were many patients who received tainted blood before testing was initiated. We are in the process of tracking down those individuals who received those transfusions to see if any have Chagas disease. So far, nobody has contracted the disease."

"You mean nobody yet!" I said.

"Of course you are right, the infection can remain dormant for a period of time. But there is another issue. While we have done testing since the first availability of the assay, the FDA currently does not mandate testing, so not all blood banks have instituted the assay," Dr. Sedor said.

"What? Why not?" was my question.

"It is an economic issue. The costs for universal testing of the blood supply may not outweigh the prevention of one infection. According to medical economist, screening for Chagas costs over $1 million dollars to produce one quality-adjusted life year or QALY. With a typical QALY cutoff of $100,000, this is a price-tag that we as the nation cannot afford."

"Unless it is you or your family member that gets the disease," I said.

"The real lesson is that blood transfusions will never be without risks. Therefore, administering blood products should be avoided as a therapeutic measure unless absolutely necessary," Dr. Sedor said. If you know you will need blood in the future, say for an elective surgical procedure, patients should consider auto-transfusions, donating blood and saving it for yourself in case it is needed," Dr. Sedor concluded.

"I certainly agree with that strategy," I told her.

*

Hugo's unused blood was processed. The plasma was put into a freezer for storage. Fresh frozen plasma is stable for many months. Soon, a portion of Hugo's donated plasma was thawed and given to a neonate undergoing cardiac surgery to repair the child's congenital heart defect. Unknown to the pediatricians, the blood that the infant received was infected with *T. cruzi*. While the operation was successful in repairing the cardiac defect, the baby acquired Chagas disease. The child developed an enlarged heart, and died a few weeks later. Postmortem samples were sent to a University hospital for examination, which revealed the presence of the deadly parasite. Doctors determined that the infant had an immature immune system that made it difficult for her to fight the infection. The family asked the blood bank who was the donor of the unit, but that information is kept confidential. Hugo never knew that it was his blood that caused the death of a child elsewhere in his town.

*

Chagas disease is named after Carlos Chagas, a Brazilian doctor who first described the disease in 1909. It is endemic in Central and South America with an estimate of over 10 million cases. With the increasing mobility of the human population, Chagas disease is spreading to rest of the world. The primary reservoirs for Trypanosoma cruzi *are the raccoon, opossums, squirrels and mice. Chagas disease can be effectively treated with azole drugs if given during the acute phase. There are currently no vaccines available although there have been some successes made for a vaccine in mouse models.*

Donated blood is tested for antibodies to T. cruzi in areas with a high rate of Chagas infections. This has substantially reduced the incidence of the disease in endemic parts of the world. In the U.S., there have only been a few documented cases of disease transmission through blood transfusions. All of these cases were in young children and elderly individuals. In addition to an antibody test, there are now molecular assays that test for the presence of the parasites. Compared to the antibody tests, these polymerase chain reaction tests can be used to determine if the disease is active and whether or not the individual is infectious. T. Cruzi can also be visualized when peripheral blood is examined under a microscope with the appropriate stain.

Improving the housing conditions has also been effective in reducing transmission from triatominae. This has been an objective of international relief organizations such as Habitat for Humanity. Interestingly, T. cruzi does not thrive very well in the Amazon's rain forest. These conditions are not conducive for the life cycle of the triatominae insect. With the deforestation of this forest, the incidence of Chagas may increase. It is somewhat ironic given that Hugo went to South America to improve the hosing conditions for Paolo and his family.

Holy Shit!

****

Gertrude was active all her life. She was smart, ambitious, and somewhat restless. She and her older sister Chase were young children during World War II. Their father died during the Battle of the Bulge in late 1944. Neither of them really knew him. Fortunately, the family was wealthy and their mother was able to keep them comfortable. Chase went to college. Her sole objective was to find a husband of means. She lived in a sorority. Chase met the man of her dreams in college and they married. He was an executive at a Wall Street firm and they lived in Greenwich, Connecticut.

Gertrude entered the same college as her sister two years later and pledged at the same sorority. But her objective was to have a career. During the late 1950s, it was extremely difficult for women to get equal employment status as men. There were very few female executives at the time. Gertrude's professors at the college told her not to set her sights too high.

"Gertrude, you are smarter than any of my male students," he once told her. "You would be a star if you were male. But there is a bias against women of child bearing age. I have seen many of my most promising former students get pregnant just as they are climbing the corporate ladder. Senior executives do not like their young stars to be out of touch for months at a time. I know it is not fair, but it is just human biology."

"That's bullshit!" Gertrude told her professor as she left his office. *I am going to be different,* she vowed to herself.

Gertrude finished college and took a job at the headquarters of a drug store chain. She started in the marketing department at the bottom. She was the only woman in the office who wasn't a secretary. She was often asked by her co-workers to get coffee, and even their dry cleaning. Gertrude put up mild resistance but did her job. She was hopeful that eventually they would see that she was more than a gopher.

Gertrude put her personal life on hold and devoted all of her time to the company. She was always among the first of her colleagues to arrive. And because the company had divisions on the West Coast, she routinely worked into the evening talking to colleagues who were on Pacific Time. Gertrude spent many Saturdays in the office too. There was no time for Gertrude to find love. Because she was rarely home, Gertrude did not have any pets. *I don't have time to a walk dog or change litter boxes,* was her justification to herself. Her only social release was visiting Chase and her family of three small children. However, when it came time to babysit, Gertrude consistently declined. The thought of changing dirty diapers was just a little too domesticated for her taste. *I'll gladly pay someone to sit these kids* she thought, but that was never necessary.

All of the hard work paid off for Gertrude. She slowly rose up the corporate ranks and she eventually became vice president of her division. But it came at the expense of her youth. Gertrude was now in her late forties and never married.

She had a few causal affairs, but it was always work first for Gertrude.

*

In the meantime, Chase's children were in college and for a while she and her husband were "empty nesters." They took the opportunity to travel abroad. But this situation didn't last long. Chase and Gertrude's mother began to suffer from dementia and needed nursing assistance. Gertrude wanted to put her into a home.

"She will get professional care there," she told her sister. Chase refused to sign the papers.

"My husband and I agree that she will live with us." Their mother lived for a few more years before dying at their home.

*

Gertrude retired at the age of 65. She moved into a senior community in White Plains near one of city's public parks. At first, it was difficult for Gertrude, having been a work-alcoholic all her life. But she found other things to do. She became active in her town's politics and was elected to the city council. She dealt with many issues including funds for the library and the renovations for the parks. One issue in particular occupied her time. Gertrude couldn't help but notice that many of the local residents do not clean up the poop left by their dogs. While there was a city ordinance against this practice, it was difficult to enforce because these dogs were often walked at night after dark. *These animals are disgusting,* she thought. Gertrude received funding from the city to set aside fenced-in areas specifically for dogs. There was resistance at first because this took space away from the children. But during the open debate on this subject, one of the mothers complained that one of their toddler's accidently fell face first into a pile and everyone was disgusted by this imagery. Gertrude had no problems getting the necessary vote after that statement.

*

A few years later, Gertrude's health began to slowly fade. Now in her seventies, she moved to a senior living community in Northern California to avoid the northeastern winters. She took daily walks in the park near her home. She was thrilled that she could do this even in the winter. In watching others, she was amazed that many people in the park were wearing full winter coats, scarfs, and wool hats. *How can these people think it is cold when it is 50 degrees out?* was her thought. *They would never survive a New England Nor' easter.* But during one rainy January, Gertrude made the mistake of not bundling up. She caught pneumonia and was hospitalized for several days. When she was discharged, she was given a prescription for oral clindamycin, a wide spectrum antibiotic. Neither she nor her doctors knew at the time that this drug would alter her gastrointestinal flora.

It was a few months later when Gertrude, who was home, slipped and fell while getting out of her bath tub. She broke a hip and needed replacement surgery. Her bones were weakened by arthritis, so she was scheduled for a total hip replacement. A cobalt metal-on-metal joint replacement was implanted. Gertrude was wheeled into the recovery room. Because of her advancing age, Gertrude was sent to a temporary assisted living facility upon her discharge from the hospital. The residents living there had a variety of different illnesses. One resident in particular had watery diarrhea and needed daily assistance with bathing. Felipe was one of the caretakers assigned to this patient. Felipe was careful in his infection control practice. He thoroughly washed his hands in between each patient encounter. On this day, however, some of the diarrhea leaked onto the bottom of his hospital tunic without his knowledge. When he went to visit Gertrude, the contaminated coat rubbed against Gertrude's bed. Gertrude became sick and returned to the hospital.

*

In the clinical laboratory, we had just instituted a new molecular test for *Clostridium difficile*, a drumstick like Gram positive bacteria. *C. difficle* produces an enterotoxin and cytotoxins that cause diarrhea and inflammation among infected patients. Diagnosis of a *C. difficile* infection is through a toxigenic culture, whereby the microorganism is cultured from stools and tested for toxin production. This is a difficult assay that takes 1-2 days to complete. But it is considered the gold standard because it is difficult to grow these microorganisms from a traditional stool culture. An assay that detects the toxin is also available. While these tests are fast, there are some cases of *C. difficle* infection that are missed. The newly implemented molecular test detects specific DNA sequences within the microorganism and is more sensitive for diagnosis.

A sample of Gertrude's stool was sent to the lab and tested. Before the result was available, one of my senior microbiology technologists, Martha, was put to the test. Having worked on this bench for many years, she had bragged to her fellow techs that she could detect a distinct odor of *C. difficle* from a stool sample. When she came near Gertrude's sample, she said to us that the patient had a *C. difficile* infection. Within an hour, the molecular test was completed. The result, of no surprise to Martha, was strongly positive. Despite her unique ability, I told Martha that we were not going to use her as a permanent *C. difficile* smell tester. The senior tech was relieved to hear that.

Gertrude was placed into an isolation ward where special precautions were taken to minimize the spread of her infection to other patients and to healthcare workers. Anyone entering her room had to wear a sterile gown, mask, and gloves which were discarded immediately after exiting the room. Gertrude was treated with a number of antibiotics including vancomycin and metronidazole. My chemistry laboratory measured the vancomycin concentration from Gertrude's blood on a regular basis to determine if she was getting the right dose. Her blood drug levels were within the accepted therapeutic range. None of the antibiotics used to treat Gertrude's infection were effective and she suffered from relapsing disease. Dr. Burlingame, an infectious disease specialist, was consulted on this case.

"None of the drugs we have tried has been successful in treating your infection," Dr. Burlingame said.

"So where do we go from here?" Gertrude asked.

"We would like to try fecal microbiota transplantation" he said.

Gertrude, who was fairly knowledgeable about medical advancements, was a little unclear what Dr. Burlingame meant. "Did you say fetal transplant? Do you mean treatment with stem cells?" was her question. Gertrude knew that stem cells were undifferentiated cells derived from embryonic tissues. They have been used experimentally to treat a variety of diseases including Alzheimer and Parkinson's disease. *Do I have one of these diseases?* She thought. Her mind was racing to different possibilities.

"No, I said fecal not fetal. We want to do a stool transplant," Dr. Burlingame replied.

"You'll have to explain this further," Gertrude said.

"From your medical record, we saw that you were recently treated with a broad spectrum antibiotic during your bout with pneumonia. While this eradicated your illness, it also sterilized your normal gastrointestinal flora. Then when you were in the nursing facility, you somehow became infected with C. *difficle*, probably from another resident. Hospitals and nursing home facilities are major sources of transmission. A microbiota transplant is a procedure to restore your colonic flora by infusing stool from a normal healthy donor."

"You are going to put someone else's poop into my body?" Gertrude couldn't believe what she was hearing.

"In essence, yes." Dr. Burlingame said matter-of-factly. He was experienced with this procedure and the response by patients when informed about this option.

Gertrude sat there for a few moments to think about what Dr. Burlingame said. "I don't know if I can do this," was her response to the doctor.

"You are acting like a child!" Dr. Burlingame stated harshly hoping to generate a positive response. "This is a life threatening infection. Thousands of people in American die from this each year. You are infected by a particularly virulent strain. You should consider yourself lucky to have access to this unique and cutting edge procedure. I believe this is your only therapeutic option remaining," the doctor said.

"I'm 75 years old. My body is failing me. I have no family, no children. I don't have much more to accomplish," she said. "I don't need to make medical history."

"Don't you have a sister, nieces, and nephews? Talk it over with them."

Dr. Burlingame left the room and Gertrude started crying. She had always been in control of all situations but she wasn't sure what to do. Some of Dr. Burlingame's statements made sense. Chase found out from Gertrude what the doctors wanted to do. When Gertrude told her sister that she wasn't going to let them do it, Chase flew in to see Gertrude.

"You've had a perversion with poop from the very beginning." Chase knew that her sister had never changed a diaper on her children or her incontinent mother. For her kids and her kid's kids, Chase was a veteran diaper changer for over 50 years now. "There is nothing disgusting about it."

Despite her best efforts, Chase was unable to convince Gertrude to proceed with the fecal transplant. Chase even volunteered to be tested and be the donor of the stool transplant. Gertrude elected to remain on antibiotics but her health declined rapidly. Gertrude passed a few days later. She was buried alongside her mother.

*

Most people view microbiology in a negative way. While it is true that many microorganisms are highly toxic, it is difficult for humans to exist without them. Scientists have reported that there is 10 times the number of microbial cells in our bodies than human cells themselves. They further opine that there may be 100 times more genes associated with microbiomes than genes found in humans. Shortly after birth, colonization with bacteria begins. By adulthood, bacteria are pervasive within our oral cavity, skin, conjunctiva, gastrointestinal and urogenital tract. A major role of bacterial organisms found in humans is the protection against the colonization of foreign potentially pathogenic microbes.

Microorganisms can also assist in digestion, nutrition through the production of essential vitamins, and activation of the immune system for host protection. The National Institute of Health initiated a multi-center study in 2008 to characterize the human microbiome from over 250 healthy individuals. To date, researchers have identified and cataloged over 10,000 microbiologic species from 15 to 18 key body sites. This work is a follow-up to the Human Genome Project, completed in 2003, whereby the entire genomic sequence of an individual was mapped.

Fecal microbiota transplantation involves identifying a healthy donor who test negative for a wide array of bacterial and parasitic infections. The fecal sample is extracted with saline, filtered, and administrated to the infected patient through an enema or nasogastric tube. Most patients with a C. difficle infection improve or recover after a single treatment. If an individual is deemed to be at high risk for a C. difficle infection, an autologous fecal sample can be provided by the donor, and stored frozen for future use on him or herself. This approach, while more physiologically appealing, may be less effective, as the patient's original flora may have predisposed the individual to the infection in the first place. Also, a pill containing processed human feces can be taken. If one doesn't think about what is inside, it may be easier to administer than an enema.

The recognition of the role that bacteria have on human health has made its way to the food industry. Many companies offer yogurt, dietary supplements, and other products that contain active cultures and promote probiotic help in preventing infections and recurrences. Whether or not this will reduce the incidence of C. difficile and other gastrointestinal infections remains to be seen.

To someone trained in science and medicine, a fecal transplant makes logical sense to me. But to others, this idea may be against religious beliefs. There are religious groups who cannot accept blood transfusions. It is unclear if there will be other religious beliefs that object to fecal transplantation.

Bugs in Space

As a young assistant professor working in Houston Texas, I had the unique opportunity to interact with astronauts and scientists at the Johnson Space Center or "JSC." One of my jobs was to evaluate prototype clinical laboratory equipment for possible deployment into the microgravity environment of space.

Astronauts and scientists live and train in and around Clear Lake Texas, a southeast suburb of Houston. One evening, my wife and I had dinner with one astronaut and his wife shortly after the crash of the Space Shuttle *Challenger* in 1986. At the time, NASA had suspended flight operations of the Shuttle program until a thorough root cause analysis was completed and corrective safety measures were implemented.

"Dr. Story Musgrave, do you have any reservations in returning to space once the program resumes," I asked my guest. Dr. Musgrave flew on the maiden voyage of the *Challenger*. His second flight on that Shuttle took place just 6 months before its crash.

"I have none, what-so-ever. We have the best people working to make this right. We'll be back and we'll be better than ever. My astronaut colleagues and I can't wait to get back into space. It has been an honor and privilege to serve NASA and our country and I will continue to do so when called."

A chill ran down my spine then and to this day. These brave men and women really do have the *"right stuff."* True to his word, Dr. Musgrave went on to fly four more times on *Discovery, Atlantis, Endeavour, and Columbia.* His last flight was in 1996 and lasted 17 days.

Like Dr. Musgrave, the scientists associated with the program are highly educated professionals with multiple advanced degrees in areas such as astrophysics, engineering and medicine. The physicians at the Space Center conduct studies on the physiologic effects of microgravity. Immediately after takeoff, astronauts experience a redistribution of body fluids towards the head. Prolonged exposure causes "space osteoporosis" a loss of calcium from the weight bearing bones of the body. There are other hormonal changes that are associated with the stress of the mission.

Astronauts are medically examined before, during, and after missions. In addition to physical and psychiatric exams, the JSC operates a full service clinical laboratory where blood, urine and body fluids of astronauts are taken on a regular basis and examined for health abnormalities. While the JSC Medical Clinic serves outpatients, the doctors there had their hands full during one mission in particular...

*

Addison Wentworth found out early what he was going to do for a living. It was traced to a cookout held during Boy Scout Camp. Addison ate undercooked chicken that was contaminated with *Salmonella.* During the night, Addison woke up and became violently ill with gastrointestinal pain and diarrhea. He made frequent trips to the camp's outhouse. The camp counselor told him to drink plenty of fluids in order to avoid dehydration. The counselor hoped that the boy's food poisoning would subside by morning. When Addison's symptoms persisted, an ambulance was called and the boy was taken to the nearest hospital. He was treated with antibiotics and released to his parents the next day.

Over the ensuing years, Addison took an interest in medical microbiology because of his childhood illness. As a senior in high school, he and his science teacher, Mr. Russell, submitted a research study to be conducted aboard NASA's space shuttle. This was part of a national competition among high school science students. Under simulated zero gravity conditions, Addison read that scientists had concluded that bacteria were more virulent. Addison posed the question, "If bacteria are hardier in space, are antibiotics also less effective?" Addison's teacher, a former medical technologist, told his student about the Kirby Bauer antibiotic susceptibility test.

"A petri dish is inoculated with specific bacteria. Paper disks soaked with antibiotics are placed onto the agar. If the bacteria are susceptible to a particular drug, there will be no bacterial growth observed around the disks. If the bacteria are resistant, it will be cloudy indicating growth around the disk," Mr. Russell said.

Addison's science proposal was selected among the tens of thousands submitted to NASA. His study was loaded and performed aboard the International Space Station. Addison and Mr. Russell watched a closed circuit broadcast of the work while it was being conducted on the Station. After the astronauts landed,

Addison, his family, and Mr. Russell were flown to Houston where the results of his study were revealed. The Chief NASA Microbiologist met with the student and teacher in a press conference.

"These are photos of Kirby-Bauer plates for *Staphylococcus* bacteria conducted in our lab on earth. Here is what happens when these same bacteria are grown over several generations in space. As you can see, there are more cloudy areas around the Kirby Bauer disks when the study was conducted in microgravity compared to the same study conducted on earth. Son, you were right, microbes ARE more virulent when grown in space." The scientist was looking directly at Addison, who was thrilled that his experiment had succeeded. After the announcement, newspaper reporters hovered around Addison to ask questions. His NASA experiment made national news. He went to Washington DC and received an award from the National Institute of Health. When he returned home, he was the toast of his high school class.

Later that year, Addison was awarded a National Merit Scholarship and upon completion of high school, he attended college the following fall. After graduating with a Bachelor's degree in biology, Addison went on to grad school and received a doctoral degree in bacteriology. After two-years of a postdoctoral fellowship, Dr. Allison Wentworth became an Assistant Professor at California State University.

Addison continued his association with NASA that started when he was a teenager. Within a few years, he and his colleagues suggested that the microgravity environment produces bacteria that behave more like those in their natural environment of the gut. He was among the first to suggest that this knowledge could be helpful in developing new vaccines. Funded by NASA grants, he conducted preliminary studies to demonstrate feasibility. Soon, he was ready to have his theories tested in space.

*

Duncan Myers was the youngest of 7 siblings. He shared a room with two other boys and it was always loud and noisy. He was considered by his parents to be an anti-claustrophobic. He loved to be in tight and confined spaces. When he played hide and seek with his older brothers, he found the best places to hide in their large old house. There was one game where Duncan stayed in his hiding place for an hour after the game had ended. He liked having a quiet place all to himself. He only came out when his mother shouted that it was dinner time. In the backyard, Duncan spent many nights camped out alone in a small pup tent. Sometimes he would take Mindy, the family's black Labrador in with him for security. It came as no surprise to his parents that Duncan, as a teenager, announced that he wanted to be an astronaut. His older brothers started teasing him.

"Yeah, and I am going to play for the Chicago Bulls," one of them said.

"Don't mind them honey," his mother told Duncan. "You can be whatever you want." She could visualize him alone in a space station orbiting the earth.

Duncan excelled in college and graduate school and received a doctoral degree in astrogeology. He landed a job at the Johnson Space Center as a research scientist. There, he befriended several of the astronauts. They encouraged him to follow his childhood dream. Duncan was in excellent mental and physical health. He hired a personal trainer to improve his conditioning. Duncan was granted an interview and underwent a series of tests. He did particularly well in the psychiatric tests. Duncan was well adjusted, knew what he wanted, and relished the idea of working and living in tight quarters remote from the rest of mankind. While he was naturally shy, being the last child of a large family, he was used to defending himself and spoke up when needed. His ability to command an audience was an important attribute for an astronaut, as he will have to speak to the public. Duncan's expertise in geology was particularly important. After two months of interviews and tests, Duncan was selected to be among the next group of NASA astronauts. Dr. Duncan Myers and the other new crew members were introduced at a press conference to a small gathering of reporters in Houston. This was a very different scene from when the original Mercury 7 Astronauts were introduced to the nation back in 1959 when there were hundreds of national and international members of the media covering the event.

Duncan spent the next 3 years training on various NASA protocols for space flight. In case of an emergency, he had to be familiar with all operations. There were countless hours of computer and mechanical simulations. He took numerous courses in a diversity of fields including physics, engineering, mathematics, computer sciences, medical science, and biomedical engineering. He was assigned as a payload specialist and was trained to perform scientific investigations. All the while, Duncan had to maintain his physical and mental conditioning. He ate right, exercised regularly, and attended psychology sessions. Not everyone is suited to be in a confined space vehicle for a prolonged period of time. When he was finally selected for a mission, his childhood dream had come true.

Dr. Duncan Myers was assigned to work with Dr. Addison Wentworth on his *Salmonella* vaccine project. Duncan spent two months in Addison's lab learning about the techniques that he was to perform at the Space Station. Both men were about the same age, married, and each had a daughter at home. They soon became good friends. When Addison and his family visited the Johnson Space Center later that year, they stayed at Duncan's home. Over dinner, both men were explaining their mission to their wives Diane Wentworth and Helena Myers, and their daughters.

"The microgravity environment of space simulates the natural movement of bacteria while it is in the human digestive tract," Addison said.

"NASA is particularly interested because in the absence of gravity, bacteria distribute evenly through the air of the space station" Duncan commented.

Addison then stated, "Studying *Salmonella* is a good first step because infections are generally from food contamination and not spread through aerosolization."

Duncan's 11-year old girl was listening intently. "I don't want my Daddy to get sick in space."

"I won't let that happen, dear," Duncan said. Then turning to his wife, he said "I will be working behind a screen and performing the studies using a glove box. I won't be directly exposed to these bacteria."

*

After months of planning and countless hours of

simulations, the day finally arrived for Duncan Myers and the four other astronauts from his mission to launch. Addison and his family joined Duncan's family and they flew to Cape Canaveral to watch the event. All of them were very nervous. While NASA has a good safety record, there will always be a risk putting men and women into space. The lift off is one of the most dangerous phases of the mission. When the rocket containing the Space Shuttle launched, there was a loud cheer from the spectators that came to witness the event. Helena was so nervous she could hardly stand. She cried at the sight of her husband leaving the earth. She had attended briefing sessions for astronaut wives in preparation for this day, but she was overcomed by her emotions. Addison was also concerned about his friend and colleague. *Godspeed, Duncan Myers* he whispered to himself.

The first 24 hours of the flight was unpleasant for Duncan Myers. He developed motion sickness with terrible nausea. He had a headache from the redistribution of fluid from his legs to his neck due to microgravity. The experienced astronauts aboard the Shuttle told him this was natural. They all experienced similar problems during their first flight. By the time they docked with the Space Station and embarked from the Shuttle, Duncan's symptoms began to subside. The next day, Duncan went about the business of living and working in space. There was a routine that had to be followed for eating, sleeping, working, exercising, having leisure time, and taking bathroom breaks. He was thoroughly trained in all of these areas. On the fourth day of the mission, he was scheduled to perform the studies designed by Dr. Addison Wentworth. The space station

McAulliffe aboard *Challenger,* and Rick Husband aboard *Columbia.*

*

Salmonella *is a rod-shaped Gram-negative bacterium. There are more than 1.2 million illnesses each year in the U.S., with more than 23,000 hospitalizations and 450 deaths reported each year. It can occur when meat and eggs contaminated with the bacteria are undercooked. The "typhoid" form of* Salmonella *produces typhoid fever. There are approximately 16 million people worldwide who are infected per year with about a 5% mortality rate. A* Salmonella *infection can be diagnosed through a blood or stool culture. Molecular techniques can also be used for diagnosis and for designation of subtypes.*

Actually there have been no space casualties due to microbiologic exposures in either the U.S. or Soviet space programs, and Duncan Myers is a fictitious character. The only biological agents permitted onboard the International Space Station are those that fall into Biosafety level 1 and 2. Agents such as Yersinia pestis *(bacteria that causes the plague),* Mycobacterium tuberculosis, *and SARS fall under level 3, while the Ebola virus falls under level 4. The Space Station does not have onboard biosafety level facilities to handle these infectious agents and investigations using these agents are not currently permitted. There are only a few Biosafety Level 4 laboratories in the U.S.*

Research studies conducted on the International Space Station have played an important role in the development of modern vaccines to Salmonella, Streptococcus, *and other infectious agents. These studies have identified key components thought to be responsible for human disease. This work has led to development of candidate vaccines. One directed against* Streptococcus pneumonia *is currently in clinical trials.*

NASA has proposed the creation of a Crew Return Vehicle for emergency use by astronauts living on the International Space Station. Numerous designs were proposed and several flying prototypes were constructed. None of these prototypes ever made it to space. Unfortunately the program was never funded and a rescue vehicle is currently not available and would not have been available for Duncan Myers.

My involvement with NASA ended with my departure from the University of Texas Medical School, Houston. Recently, I was in the unenviable position of having to give a dinner lecture after Mark Kelly, a former NASA astronaut. Kelly talked about his combat missions in Desert Storm, his four Space Shuttle missions, and the horrific events surrounding the assassination attempt of his wife, Gabrielle Giffords, the former Congresswoman from Arizona. After his talk, I had to bring the lab medicine audience back to earth with a discussion on cardiac markers.

Feline Folly

Felicia grew up on a small farm in central California. Their land was rather hilly so her father raised livestock. Felicia's mother had a large vegetable garden.

"Our vegetables almost grow themselves," her mother would say to Felicia and her older sisters. "We live in one of the most fertile places on earth. The weather is good and there is plenty of sunshine." It was true. California produces nearly half of America's fruits, nuts and vegetables. Among Felicia's daily chores was tending to the vegetable garden. While her sisters hated weeding, Felicia liked working in the earth with her bare hands.

There were plenty of domesticated animals living on the farm. Their farm cats came in all shapes and sizes. Her father had them around to reduce the rodent population. Some lived outside. Many never left the house. Felicia loved her cats. She was still in grade school when her sisters were in high school. When the older girls started dating, she was often left alone to play with her feline friends. Little did Felicia know that it would be her own beloved pets that would cause her harm!

*

Felicia went to community college to get certified as a

real estate agent. She went to work in a small city not far from her family's farm. She rented a house on the outskirts of town. There were perks associated with being a real estate agent. Her rental property had some land and was inexpensive. She had seen the MLS listing before it became public, took an afternoon off to see the place, and signed the lease that night. It came to nobody's surprise that Felicia cultivated her own vegetable garden. She also took three of the friendlier cats from the family farm to her house as pets. Their names were Curry, Mango and Chabade. These cats were confined to the house and they were not allowed outside.

Through her work, Felicia met many people looking for homes. While most were married, she occasionally had single males as clients. Many of the younger men she encountered were successful junior executives, lawyers, or doctors. Meeting new people was another advantage of her occupation. Felicia was attracted to one man in particular, Noah, who was a certified public accountant. Noah lived in an apartment downtown and wanted to have more space. He made several appointments with Felicia to look at houses and property to purchase. None of the listings that she showed him were suited to Noah. They were either too small, too far from work, or too expensive. There was a terrible smell in the neighborhood of one property they went to. After a while, Felicia began to think that Noah was more interested in her than in serious house hunting. Felicia found Noah attractive and didn't mind these failures. But he was a client and she had to keep her personal feelings private. But then one day, he finally asked her out on a date.

"It is against our company's policy to date clients," she

told him.   Felicia saw that Noah's body language showed immediate disappointment. *That was a stupid thing to say*, she thought. *Think of something to say fast or you will lose him.*

"If we turn your search over to one of my colleagues, then you won't be my customers," Felicia said. With that said, Noah's demeanor perked up again.

Noah and Felicia saw each other regularly for the next several months. While Noah was initially looking to buy a house, his relationship with Felicia put this notion on the back burner. They began dating and soon, Noah moved into Felicia's house. She loved Noah and hoped that they would eventually get married.

Six months later, Felicia became pregnant. By then it was clear that they were meant for each other and they made wedding plans. Noah had only a few relatives and they lived back East. Most of Felicia's relatives lived nearby. So the wedding was held at Felicia's family farm.   It was a small country-style wedding. One of Felicia's sisters was the bridesmaid. A cousin from New York, who grew up with Noah, was the best man. After the wedding, the couple went to Kona on the Big Island of Hawaii for their honeymoon. They returned to their home two weeks later.

The first two trimesters of Felicia's pregnancy were uneventful. She underwent regular prenatal checkups and learned very early that she was carrying a boy. During the beginning of her last trimester however, Felicia got sick. She had a fever and the lymph glands around her neck and under her armpits were swollen. Felicia's obstetrician, Dr. Eleanor Lamb gave her a thorough examination.   She concluded that she had the flu and that she needed bed rest. While that seemed to be the most likely explanation, Noah was not convinced. He went on the internet and investigated sicknesses that were common during pregnancy. He read about preeclampsia, which affects 5-8% of all pregnancies and can lead to maternal death. When he learned that preeclampsia is most common among women during their first pregnancies, he became real concerned and called Dr. Lamb.

"Preeclampsia is a rapidly progressing condition that is characterized by headaches, high blood pressure and excretions of proteins in the urine. It often begins during the first 20 weeks of pregnancy," Dr. Lamb stated. "We checked her blood pressure and did a dipstick urinalysis on her. She was normal on both counts. I recommend you purchase an at-home blood pressure monitoring device. I don't recommend a wrist or finger stick device, but that you buy a cuff-style upper arm monitor like the ones we use here. I have provided a list of approved devices. My nurse can train you on how to operate it. I will also prescribe urine dipsticks that you can use to check her urine."

Noah felt much better now that he had some control and responsibility towards Felicia's health. He bought the blood pressure device and test strips and urine cups and tested his wife regularly over the next few days. He became concerned again when she did not improve despite the fact that her blood pressure and urine protein levels were consistently normal. He called Dr. Lamb and this time, asked for an appointment.

"She is still very sick. Her glands are still swollen. There must be something else wrong. What can we do?" Noah asked.

"Causes of swollen glands that are unresponsive to antibiotics include malignant diseases such as Hodgkin's lymphoma. We may need to perform a lymph node biopsy to diagnosis this disease." When Noah heard this, the blood quickly drained from his face and he became pale and ashen.

The doctor thought for a moment and said, "There is another possible explanation. Do you have cats at home?"

*

My chemistry laboratory does serology testing to detect antibodies to infectious diseases. We received a serum sample from Dr. Lamb on Felicia labeled "TORCH Panel." There were no individual tests listed on this requisition but the identification of the specific tests was unnecessary. Working with obstetricians, the clinical laboratory as a profession designed a panel of tests to be used on pregnant women who present with specific symptoms of an infection. The four tests included in the panel include toxoplasmosis, rubella or German measles, cytomegalovirus or CMV, and herpes simplex virus.

"An infected woman can transmit these microorganisms to their unborn infant," I told one of my medical technology students who wanted to know more about the panel. "There can be serious consequences from contracting these diseases."

As an exercise, I asked Dr. Arlene Dole, one my lab medicine residents to explain the clinical manifestations of these infections to the newborn. "Neonates infected with CMV or "C" can have seizures, hearing loss, vision loss and mental retardation. A rubella infection or "R" can cause respiratory distress, blindness, and deafness. A child with congenital herpes or "H" can develop seizures, respiratory problems, but also inflammation of the brain, lungs, liver and kidneys. Deaths can occur in infants whose infection is unrecognized or untreated" she said to the student. She purposely waited for me to disclose the result of the "TO" of the TORCH panel tests.

"This woman produced a negative result for the "RCH" tests from the TORCH panel" I said after examining our report. "But she is positive for toxoplasmosis."

"Toxoplasmosis is caused by a protozoan parasite called *Toxoplasma gondii*. It is transmitted to humans through consumption of raw or undercooked meat such as pork, lamb, or deer that is contaminated with this parasite" Dr. Dole said.

"Someone who owns outdoor cats can also get infected. Cats who catch and eat mice and rats contaminated with *Toxoplasma* can host these parasites within their bodies. Some of the protozoa are excreted into their feces. Not cleaning cat litter boxes on a daily basis can expose a human to this parasite. Individuals who are particularly susceptible are those who have weak immune systems such as patients with HIV infections, who have had an organ transplant, or women who are pregnant."

"Our assay detects the IgG antibodies to Toxo. It usually appears within 1 to 2 months after exposure and remains positive for life. There is also an IgM antibody test can help us determine if she was exposed recently. The IgM antibody appears in blood before the IgG antibody and disappears from her blood within a few months. Her immune cells gradually convert from producing IgM to the IgG antibody. We don't have this assay available here. I will contact the patient's doctor to find out if she wants this test done and if so, we will send it to a lab in California that specializes in this testing.

*

The positive toxoplasmosis laboratory result was

reported to Dr. Lamb who called Noah and Felicia to reveal the results. She also told them that they would be getting a visit from Evian Holmes, an infectious disease investigator from the Department of Public Health. Evian arrived to their home and was let inside. Immediately, several of Felicia's cats came to greet the visitor. Evian told them that it was his job to investigate how Felicia might have been exposed to *Toxoplasma gandii*. He explained the potential role that cats have in spreading this infection from rodents to people. He questioned Felicia and Noah about how these cats lived in their household.

"You're not going to take away my cats are you?" Felicia said while holding back her tears.

"Felicia, let's hear what the man has to say," Noah said calming Felicia down. The couple told the investigator that none of the cats were allowed to go outside.

"Our cats are housebound. We don't have any mice in the house. " Felicia said, somewhat defensibly, thinking that HER cats could never cause them harm. Noah confirmed this fact. Evian looked at the three overweight pets and concluded that they had plenty of food at home and no reason to follow their natural hunting instincts. *Then how did Felicia get infected?* was Evian's next thought.

"Are there other cats that live outside in the neighborhood?" Evian asked.

"Well, yes, many of them come over to the house. Our cats have staring, snorting, and growling fights through the window. But there is never any physical contact. I make sure that THAT doesn't happen," Felicia said.

Evian sought permission to go outside with Noah and

Felicia and look around the property. Around the side yard, he saw am immaculate vegetable garden with tomatoes, cucumbers, peppers, and lettuce. Walking toward it, he asked, "is this your garden Felicia?"

"Yes, I do all of the watering, pruning, and weeding myself," Felicia said proudly, while at the same time passing a quick glare to her husband. Evian ignored the innuendo that Noah didn't share in this responsibility.

"Do you wear gloves when you work?" Evian asked.

"No." Felicia said. "I grew up on a farm. I like the feel of soil on my hands. What does all this mean?"

Evian was writing down all of the details. When he finished he explained his theory to the couple. "Cats can be infected with toxoplasmosis if they catch and eat rodents who are infected with this parasite. Their bodies are good hosts for toxoplasmosis. After a few weeks, infected cats begin to excrete oocysts into their stool. These spores can survive in the earth for up to a year. Cats like to poop in gardens because the soil is loose and they can bury their stools easily."

Felicia began to think that working in the garden while pregnant might not have been a good idea.

"I suspect a neighboring cat was infected and then deposited these oocytes into your garden through its feces. You may have been exposed while working in the garden," Evian concluded.

"I'm getting a little nauseous hearing this," Felicia responded.

"You may have also been exposed to Toxo while you were a child growing up on a farm. Roughly 10% of women of childbearing age are positive. The infection can lie dormant for many years and only cause sickness during a time when you have a reduced immunity. Pregnancy is one of the conditions that can cause acute sickness. However, in your case, your IgM antibodies were also positive in your blood. This indicates that you were more likely exposed recently. This is why I came out to inspect your household today."

Felicia was treated with spiramicyn, an antibiotic to reduce her symptoms and in hopes of reducing the spread of her infection to her unborn child. To determine if Felicia's fetus was infected, Dr. Lamb ordered an amniocentesis. This is when a large long needle is inserted into Felicia's abdomen and a small amount of fluid from her gestational sac is removed. This sample was tested for the toxoplasmosis parasite using molecular techniques.

Two weeks later, Felicia gave birth to a baby boy. The baby was born a few weeks premature but was otherwise healthy. The couple named him Randall. A portion of her placenta and umbilical cord blood was retained and sent to the lab for testing. Randall had no symptoms of toxoplasmosis at birth. When all of the lab tests came back, he was diagnosed as having congenital toxoplasmosis. Felicia and Noah were in Dr. Lamb's office when they were told.

Felicia started to cry when she heard the news. "What does this mean for my child?" Felicia asked Dr. Lamb.

"We will treat Randall with a combination of pyrimethamine, sulfadiazine, and folic acid, alternating with spiramycin. Your baby could have some liver disease, vision problems and mental disabilities. I am recommending a pediatrician who has experience with this infection. He will keep close watch on Randall for the first few months and years. He will also be planning a series of CT scans of his brain and vision tests as he gets older," Dr. Lamb stated.

*

Randall did not suffer any notable neurological sequelae during his childhood, but he was a hyperactive child and was diagnosed with attention deficit disorder. He was treated with Ritalin. As a teenager, he developed signs of obsessive compulsive disorder. Noah read that some children with toxoplasmosis have an increased risk towards suicide. Both of these problems have been associated with parents diagnosed with congenital toxoplasmosis. Noah and Felicia talked openly with their son about this. He showed no signs of depression. Felicia remained positive for IgG antibodies but remained asymptomatic for the disease. Noah and Felicia did not have any more children. When their cats died of old age, the couple decided not to replace them.

*

Toxoplasma gondii *was first described in 1908 in rodents and rabbits. It was not described as a human pathogen until the early 1940s. In 1948, the first serological test was described by Sabin and Feldman, a test that is still used today. The highest rate of* Toxoplasma gondii *infections are in Latin America at 50-80%. Parts of Eastern and Central Europe, the Middle East, Southeast Asia and Africa can have rates up to 60%. Unlike some countries such as France and Uruguay, The American College of Obstetrics and Gynecology has not recommended routine screening for toxoplasmosis or CMV among pregnant women because it is not cost-effective in America, and because our laboratory tests can have a* significant rate of false positive results.

Between 500 and 5000 cases of congenital toxoplasmosis are reported in the U.S., with about 750 deaths per year. Half of these infections are due to consumption of contaminated meats by mothers. Pregnant women should avoid eating raw and undercooked meat. They should also avoid handling cat feces, at least without gloves. Unwashed hands can transmit the parasite when handling and consuming contaminated food. There have been studies that suggest that women with toxoplasmosis antibodies are more likely to have baby boys than girls (e.g., 72% in one Czech study). The cause of this observation is largely unknown.

A toxoplasmosis infection that occurs in rodents causes them to alter their behavior in a manner that makes them more conducive to be caught by cats. The rats and mice exhibit more activity and exploratory behavior that can attract the attention of cats. Also, cats usually mark their "territory" from other cats through urination. Toxoplasma-infected rats and mice become less sensitive to cat body and urine odors than uninfected rodents.

While cats can be loving and affectionate, like any animal, there are risks to humans. In actual practice, investigations as to the source of infections as described in this story are not conducted.

Black Tar

Ramon lived in a small border town near Nogales, Arizona. He
did well in high school, and had a natural understanding for the
intricacies of science. Ramon wanted to go to college in the
United States but his family was poor and they didn't have the
money to pay for tuition. Instead, shortly after high school, he
took a job as a maintenance man and janitor at a local junior
college. At night, he had full access to the school's library and
the internet, and the chemistry classroom laboratory. While he
had never experimented with recreational drugs, he was curious
to learn more about what drugs some of the neighborhood kids
were taking. So one night, he searched for street names of
"Goma," and "Tootsie Roll" and found what he was looking for.
Upon reading a procedure published in 1874, Ramon learned
how to synthesize the drug using common chemical reagents
found in the college's chemistry laboratory.

The starting material is morphine so he asked his father
if he would get him some. He complained to him that the
physical nature of his job was giving him muscular aches and
pains. Ramon was never in trouble and his father didn't question
his only son. His father went to the neighborhood pharmacy and

bought the morphine pills. The pharmacist was an old friend and sold narcotics like codeine and morphine to local residents without a prescription. Officially, all sales required a doctor's script. But for some of his clients, he sold analgesic drugs under-the-counter and at a discount, in order to save these people some money by not seeing a doctor. He trusted that his clients would not sell them on the black market.

In the school's chem lab, Ramon dissolved morphine tablets into vinegar and boiled the solution using a Bunsen burner for several hours under a hood. When the mixture was completely dry, the residue was a black tarry goo when cooled. Ramon then mixed in some coffee grounds and dirt to dilute the potency of the product. After the synthesis was completed, Ramon thoroughly cleaned up the lab so that the next day, there was no trace of his work.

Ramon went to see Juan, one of his drug-addicted friends and told him to try some of the stuff he had just made. Juan was a little older and taller, but he respected Ramon because he was smart, did well in school and believed that Ramon had no reason to harm him. Juan put a small amount of the tar onto a tablespoon, added water, and heated the spoon over a match. When the goop melted, he waited a few minutes for the liquid to cool down to room temperature. Juan then took a syringe from his pocket, loaded the liquefied drug through the needle, and injected it directly into his veins. Juan sat back and enjoyed the high from the drug.

After a few minutes, Juan responded. "Ah! This is good shit, man. Where did you get this?"

"I made it in the lab. There is plenty more where that

comes from."

"I know a guy in the states who can push this stuff. If you have more, we can talk to him," Juan said. "You'll make a lot of money."

"I'm not looking to sell this. I was just curious to learn about it. Besides, I don't want to addict any of our neighborhood kids. That would be wrong."

"No worries dude. This stuff is sent to California. Who cares what happens to those rich kids anyway?" Was Juan's response.

Ramon resisted at first, but then he realized that the extra money could be used for his school tuition. So he made additional batches and sold Tootsie Rolls to Juan on a regular basis for the next few months. He never told his father about his "business." Just that he needed a regular supply of morphine for his "ailments." Ramon saved enough money and soon enrolled into the junior college. Ramon studied hard and earned straight A's. As a former maintenance man for the school, his personal history attracted a lot of local attention when he completed his associate degree. Ramon was awarded a full scholarship at a four-year university to complete the last two years of college. Once he received the acceptance letter, he stopped producing black tar and broke off all ties with Juan. His former childhood acquaintance was not happy that his drug supply ended and he threatened Ramon. Fortunately for Ramon, Juan got into an argument with a local junkie a few weeks later, as Juan was now pushing drugs locally. Juan was stabbed in the stomach with a knife and he bled to death in a back alley.

Nobody ever found out Ramon's relationship with Juan

or what he was doing in the school's chem lab. Ramon never knew where his product went or what happen to the people who used it. Now that Juan was gone, all traces of his former illicit activity were erased.

*

Joanna had been in and out of prison and drug rehabilitation centers for most of her adult life. Joanna was very attractive in her youth. Her father abandoned the family and the death of her mother while she was a teenager left her alone with no adult supervision. Joanna started out smoking crack cocaine and methamphetamine with friends. After years of use, her face and body aged quickly. She developed skin lesions and her teeth rotted out. Eventually she became an intravenous heroin user. As such, she became a "regular" at the General Hospital. She would be found on the street unresponsive with pinpoint pupils and depressed respiration. She would be treated with naloxone which quickly reversed her symptoms. But because of her addiction to heroin, she suffered from withdrawal symptoms that included headaches, nausea, vomiting.

During one of her regular visits, I received a call from Dr. Evan Frederickson, an ED resident asking for our help in drawing blood on Joanna. Her veins had scarred from her regular IV drug use to the point that there was no viable place to insert the needle. Because of her diarrhea, the ED staff needed to know if Joanna was dehydrated. They also needed vascular access to administer saline. When my phlebotomist, who is experienced with collecting blood from drug addicts, failed to get blood on Joanna, Dr. Frederickson said he had no choice but to take out the "bone drill." This was new to us so I asked to witness the procedure.

"We have this new drill that taps directly into the patient's bone marrow. Now we have vascular access to both deliver needed drugs to the patient, while at the same time, have body fluids available for clinical laboratory testing." Dr. Fredrickson showed me the drill and needle. "We can also administer fluids through this route."

"This looks excruciatingly painful," I remarked.

"Yes, the pain can be worse than injuries suffered by the patient herself. But we use a local anesthetic," he concluded.

Dr. Frederickson applied a local anesthetic, lidocaine, onto Joanna's skin and inserted the needle. She did not feel any pain. Osseous fluid was aspirated and sent to my lab for electrolytes testing. We hadn't yet validated lab procedures for bone marrow fluid. It would be difficult to get volunteers for this procedure. However, literature studies showed that for sodium and potassium, the values are nearly identical to what is found in serum. We performed the test and the results were reported to Dr. Frederickson over the phone.

After three days, Joanna's opiate withdrawal symptoms began to wane and she wanted to leave. Dr. Fredrickson told Joanna that he was going to send her to a methadone rehabilitation program.

"You want to get off heroin, right?" he asked.

"Yes. I do want to be free of my addiction but I can't help myself doc, Joanna said.

"The clinic will give you free methadone, which is a drug that blocks the effects of heroin, and it will eliminate your craving for the drug. If you don't take heroin, you won't get withdrawal symptoms. That's a fair trade right?" Joanna nodded her head.

Dr. Frederickson continued. "The clinic will also have drug counselors who are there to help you be drug free. But you must listen to them and take the methadone when they tell you. They will test your urine on a regular basis to be sure you are taking your medication."

My laboratory does testing for methadone from patients seen in the clinic. Joanna was compliant with her visits, and her urine tested positive each week.

About a year later, a sales rep was in my office explaining this new drug test. "We can now test for the methadone metabolite without reactivity towards methadone," he said to me.

"Why is that important?" I asked. "We already test for the parent drug itself."

"As you know, patients must test positive for methadone if they are to remain in the program and continue to get the drug. But a patient can fool the drug test by scraping some of the powder from the drug directly into the urine sample to be tested to produce a positive test, and sell the rest on the street. Methadone itself can produce a physiologic high. The absence of the methadone metabolite allows doctors to conclude that the drug was not in the subject's blood since the liver is needed to produce the metabolite that is excreted into urine."

"Very clever. So we should test for both the parent and metabolite to detect this situation," I stated.

"Yes," was his emphatic response. The sales rep had been well schooled by his company. By ordering two lab tests, their sales and profits would increase.

We implemented this dual urine methadone drug test

and looked for cases where there was a discrepancy between results. We found that when the methadone result was positive, the metabolite was also always positive. Since "drug diversion" was apparently not happening, this led me to reconsider the value of this approach. But I vowed to continue the testing for a few months more. Then about 6 weeks later, a tech in my lab alerted me that we had a discordant result for the two methadone urine tests on a patient. I looked at the name and recognized it from before. Joanna's urine was positive for methadone and negative for the metabolite. We contacted the methadone clinic to inform them of our suspicion that Joanna may have stopped taking methadone.

"It is possible that Janice is selling drug instead of taking it. We need to confront her with the evidence," I told the methadone clinic staff.

"We'll contact her right away. If she has stopped taking methadone, she may be back on heroin," was the response by the nurse at the clinic.

It was difficult to find Joanna because she was homeless and would stay at different shelters. When she was located, it was too late. Joanna had stopped taking her methadone. Without methadone to block the effects of heroin, she was able to get high and went on a binge. She was found in the alley near downtown and was near death. When she was brought into the General's ED and examined, the staff noted a large abscess on her inner thigh where she apparently had made her injections. Dr. Frederickson was called to duty. He in turn called the California Poison Control Center.

"I have a 45-year old female with an overdose of heroin."

Just prior to the call, Dr. Frederickson sent a urine sample to my toxicology lab where we confirmed the presence of both 6-acetylmorphine or 6-MAM and morphine. Dr. Frederickson learned from us that 6-MAM was the major human metabolite of heroin. "She has a necrotizing fasciitis on her upper leg. We think she is using black tar heroin. How can we confirm that the heroin was the source of the bacterium that caused this problem?"

The specialist at the poison center responded. "The California Department of Public Health Microbial Diseases Laboratory has a mouse bioassay. When a portion of the patient's serum is injected into mice, they will develop signs and symptoms of botulism if *Clostridium botulinum* bacteria are present in the sample. Another set of mice are injected with the patient's serum along with botulinum antitoxin. If these animals do not develop an infection, this confirms a diagnosis of botulism."

A call was placed to the microbiology lab and serum samples from Joanna were sent. Joanna was treated with antitoxin before the test results were available as a precautionary measure. A day later, the test came out positive indicating that Joanna had a botulism infection. But because of her delayed arrival to the ED, the treatment was started too late. Joanna died that afternoon from her infection. Dr. Frederickson and I were distraught because she appeared to be on the road to recovery, but something happened. Upon interviewing some of her acquaintances at the shelter, the rehabilitation clinic learned that Joanna was seeing another homeless person named Tad. In reviewing the clinic records, they learned that Tad was a patient but was thrown out of the clinic because of drug diversion. Evidently Tad taught Joanna on how to pass a urine drug test. He did that because he wanted to sell black tar heroin onto Joanna. He told her that his supply was much cheaper than the heroin she used to buy. Joanna saved up money by retrieving bottles and cans from the neighborhood and recycling them for cash.

The black tar heroin originated from Juan. Ramon, who made the drug, never knew the damage that his "science experiment" caused. It is easy in retrospect to see that Ramon and Tad made bad choices in their lives and they had affected the lives of others like Joanna. But Joanna herself was the victim of bad personal choices.

*

The bacteria Clostridium botulinum *produces a neuro-chemical called "botulinum toxin type B." This toxin can cause a flaccid paralysis or muscle weakness. Botulism is normally associated with the ingestion of food contaminated with* Clostridium. *For example, botulism has caused illness in people eating homemade canned goods that were not heated hot enough to kill the spores, or the cans were improperly sealed. A less common cause of botulism is due to the intravenous use of contaminated black tar heroin. When dirt is used to dilute black tar after its production, it can contain naturally occurring* Clostridium *spores that can infect an unsuspecting individual. Most cases of black tar botulism have occurred in California.*

The microorganism Clostridium tetani *also produces a potent poison termed "tetanus toxin." While tetanus can also lead to paralysis, it is more associated with muscle spasms of the trunk, limb, and jaws. Like botulinum, spores can be found in the soil. Unlike many other types of bacterial infections,* Clostridium *is not transmitted between individuals through blood or through the air.*

Heroin is still used as a pharmacologic agent, particularly in

117

the United Kingdom. It is produced from the dual acetylation of morphine. When black tar heroin is produced in a clandestine garage chemistry lab, the use of impure chemicals can result in an incomplete acetylation reaction. This leads to a high concentration of mono-acetyl morphine, the intermediate metabolite. This 6-MAM compound is a more potent form of heroin. So in addition to the botulism infection, Joanna was unsuspectingly injecting a more potent drug. Both were responsible for her death.

Osseous fluid collection is not commonly used in hospitals today. At the General, however, we have a large population of drug addicts that necessitates the rare use of this device.

Botulism is considered by U.S. Homeland Security as a biological weapon, although it has not yet been used in this manner. A vaccine has been developed by the Centers for Disease Control and Prevention to protect workers and military personnel against exposures. The vaccine is not approved for use by the Food and Drug Administration and is not available to protect recurrent heroin addicts like Joanna. A tetanus vaccine is widely available and routinely used, and as such, tetanus is a rare disease in the U.S. today.

Sweet Flies

After a few weeks of an Indian summer, a weather front blew in so it was a cold and rainy night in the city. On these occasions, we see many homeless people crowding into the emergency room of the General. They come in with a variety of symptoms. Some feign abdominal pain. Others come in with severe headaches. Most are just seeking shelter and a hot meal, if for only one night.

"We have one fellow, Hector, who often presents with chest pain on nights like this. His blood is consistently positive for cardiac troponin," Dr. Harold Fundus, an ER attending told me once. Troponin is a test we do in the lab that is used to diagnosis a heart attack. "But he always rules out for myocardial infarction, and we send him on his way the next day."

When I was told this, we took a sample of his blood and did a study to determine if he had an antibody that interfered with our troponin test. "Hector knows that if he pretends to have chest pain, a positive troponin result will get him admitted to the hospital. Your staff should know that he is just trying to get a warm bed for the night."

"That may be true, but what if one time he really is having a heart attack? We have to presume his symptoms are real and treat him accordingly," Dr. Fundus said.

Hector was there the night another homeless male was BIBA. This is ER jargon for "Brought In By Ambulance. Hector watched from his ER bed in the hallway as the unconscious man on the ambulance gurney was wheeled past him and directly into the triage room of the ER. Most homeless have not bathed for many days or even weeks and have offensive body odors. This man's clothes were soaked with his urine. But instead of the pungent odor, his urine had more of a fruity aroma. That pleasant smell in the air didn't last long. When the man's clothing was removed, his butt and thighs were covered with feces. The triage room was especially ripe on this night. The man did not have any identification among his possessions. So until he became conscious and could be questioned, the ED staff assigned him the temporary name, "Trauma: Giraffe." They also listed his age 125 years. This unusual age basically informed the other ED staff that his real age was yet unknown.

Dr. Harold Fundus was on duty with one of the ER nurses. From outside the room, he told the nurse, "We need blood gases, electrolytes, CBC, and coags. Put in a Foley and send urine off for a urinalysis." The nurse entered the room with the necessary supplies on a small cart. She first drew blood into a syringe from a catheter in his neck. She then took blood from a vein in his arm. She then went to work on establishing a Foley catheter by inserting the long catheter through the opening of his penis and down his shaft and into his bladder. The other end was attached to a urine collection bag attached to the bottom of the gurney. Within a few minutes, Giraffe's urine began to flow via gravity into the bag. A valve on the bottom of the bag was opened and a small amount of urine was dripped into a specimen cup. The cup was capped, labeled, and delivered to the lab for a urinalysis. Dr. Fundus was pretty sure he knew what was wrong with the patient but needed laboratory confirmation for his final diagnosis.

*

Gary Piazza was not the college type. He saw the ads while in high school and joined the Army right after graduation. He had not done much traveling outside of his hometown in rural Kansas and was excited "to see the world." He was sent to Fort Jackson in Columbia, South Carolina where he spent 10 weeks in basic training. He chose infantry school for advanced training and was sent to Fort Benning in Columbia, Georgia. Within 6 months, Gary graduated and was given a brief furlough to visit his home. When that ended, he was sent to Iraq as part of the post-war peace keeping force.

Gary spent two years at an Army base outside of Bagdad. He was near the front lines but never had to fire his weapon against the enemy. He did, however, witness the death of someone he befriended while deployed. The casualty was an American soldier from neighboring Missouri, who was killed when the truck he was driving ran over a land mine. Gary was in the vehicle behind his friend and witnessed the explosion. *That could easily have been me* was his thought. Gary was very disturbed at the death of his friend and his own brush with death. He sought counseling from Army psychiatrists. After several visits, the doctors diagnosed him as having post-traumatic stress syndrome and recommended that Private Piazza be given an honorable discharge from the Army.

Gary went home to Kansas. It was a difficult time for

him. Although he was still young, just 22 years old, he wasn't interested in going back to school. He had little motivation in finding a job. He saw doctors who tried to help him with his depression by prescribing various drugs. He tried them for a while but he suffered diarrhea and dizziness, and stopped taking them. His only solace was alcohol. After 5 years of living a hard life, his parents gave up on him and kicked him out of the house. He drifted from town to town taking on odd jobs and working his way to California. He eventually settled in San Francisco where he worked as a laborer. However, he spent most of his pension from the Army on alcohol and eventually lived on the streets.

One day, Gary was sleeping next to a group of other homeless men who were coughing and sneezing. Needless to say, Gary caught the flu from these people. Gary suffered abdominal pain, and was weak, and thirsty. His "colleagues" gave him water out of a drinking fountain from a neighboring park. This caused him to urinate frequently. That night, he passed out in an alley full of garbage cans and refuse. It was the next morning that someone found him down and called for an ambulance. It was clear that he wasn't just sleeping.

*

We equipped the General's emergency room with a blood gas and electrolyte analyzer. Within 10 minutes of blood collection, Dr. Fundus had the result that Gary's or Giraffe's, blood showed that he was profoundly acidotic. He also had a low concentration of carbon dioxide and a glucose concentration that was 8-times the normal limit. Gary Piazza was in a coma due to diabetic ketoacidosis, or "DKA." This occurs when the body's demand for insulin in processing glucose exceeds the capacity of the pancreas to produce this vital hormone. Dr. Fundus administered an injection of insulin which caused his glucose levels to quickly drop. About 45 minutes later, other laboratory reports were ready that confirmed this diagnosis. His sodium and chloride concentrations were increased due to dehydration. His urine contained ketones which caused his breath to have a fruity odor. Most of the other laboratory results were within normal limits.

After a few days, Gary was discharged from the hospital. He was sent to a shelter where he received clean clothes, hot meals and hot showers. He was also trained to give himself insulin injections on a regular basis. Unfortunately, Gary was not compliant with his medications. About 10 days after his first hospitalization, Gary was back in the emergency department with similar symptoms as before. He was having another bout of DKA. Dr. Fundus was back on duty and asked the ER staff for collection of blood and urine as before. The staff remembered Giraffe from his prior visit and they didn't need to use an alias name this time.

The nurse entered the room to remove Gary's clothes and to prepare him for the phlebotomy. She looked at Gary's face and yelled. "Oh my god!" Upon hearing this, Dr. Fundus came into the room, still putting on his glove when he saw the reason for her surprise.

"There is something moving inside his nares," she said to Dr. Fundus as she pointed to the patient's nose. Sure enough there WAS something wriggling in the man's nose. Dr. Fundus took out forceps and carefully widened the patient's nostril. They were astonished to see maggots slowly inching their way out of his nostrils. Common house flies must have been attracted to the high sugar concentrations found in his nasal fluid during his first visit to the ED. Because he was living in squalor, there were plenty of flies in the area. Attracted to the fruity aroma and high sugar content in his nasal fluid due to his diabetic ketoacidosis, a few flies flew in to his nose while he was unconscious and deposited hundreds of eggs into the moist media. Over the next week, some of these eggs turned into larvae and were squirming in his nose. Gary hardly noticed because he was in a constant state of drunkenness. Because of alcohol abuse, the social workers kicked him out of the shelter when he got sober, and he was back onto the street. Gary's nasal maggots were ready to emerge by the time of his second ED visit. Dr. Fundus pulled out several larvae from both nostrils with the forceps.

"Get me specimen cups and some sterile saline solution," he said calmly to his nurse. Dr. Fundus removed several more worms from Gary's nose with forceps and placed them into a cup. With the saline, Dr. Fundus flushed each nostril and dripped the solution into a separate specimen cup. When finished the cups were labeled and all of the blood samples, worms, and nasal aspirates were sent to the lab.

*

When we received the samples, we had never before seen anything labeled with a patient's name and the word "maggot" on it. A few minutes later, Dr. Fundus called us and explained what he wanted. One of our microbiology lab technologists, David Carter was given the assignment to determine which type of fly had infested Gary's nose. This was important in determining the lifespan of the insect and from there, deduce when the infestation took place. He contracted an entomologist at the Natural History Museum for advice. They told him that they cannot identify the species of the fly unless it is an adult. So they gave him instructions on how to grow the larvae into mature insects. David put the larvae onto a blood agar plate for incubation. He was also instructed to put wood chips into the Petri dish, to simulate a ground or dirt atmosphere. David monitored the progress of the experiment and could see that the maggots had burrowed into the nutritious media. Within a few days pupae appeared in the Petrie dish. These reddish brown structures were immobile in the agar. David thought that they were dead. The next day, the infectious disease team, who had heard about the nostril infestation, wanted to see the pupae-containing dish. David put the plate onto a projecting microscope, and shined a bright light onto the stage to show the image. After a few seconds, one pupa began to move. Then the doctors were astounded to watch an adult fly emerge from the pupae right in front of their eyes! Apparently, the heat from the lamp stimulated the emergence of the insect. At the time, the Petrie dish was covered with a clear lid so the fly was trapped inside. Upon seeing this, one student said, "This reminds me of my biology class when we used to breed Drosophila." We were all reminded of lab studies we conducted on fruit flies during our genetics class. After showing the dish around and taking photos of the fly, the dish cover was removed and the mature fly did what nature had intended for it. It flew away.

*

Gary Piazza was never told that he was harboring maggots in his nose. He survived his second bout of DKA and returned to the shelter. Realizing that he needed to take better care of his health, this time, he was compliant with his insulin prescription. Gary sought counseling from the VA Hospital for his post-traumatic stress syndrome. He was also given antidepressant drugs. These psychiatrists were more experienced with his form of depression and were more successful in getting him back on track than his previous doctors had been.

*

The U.S. Department of Housing and Urban Development (HUD) estimates that there are some 610,000 homeless individuals living on the street although unofficial estimates have listed this figure to be as high as 3.5 million. It is impossible to obtain exact figures. Many of these homeless live in cities that have warm climates like the Southern and Western States. According to HUD, roughly 20% of the homeless suffer from some sort of mental illness such as schizophrenia, bipolar disorder or severe depression. Getting medical treatment for these individuals has been an objective of each of the last several Presidential Administrations.

Maggots are the larva of house flies. They are used as bait by fisherman, particularly those who ice fish. Maggots have been used for centuries for medical treatment. This is possible because they do not harm healthy tissue. Disinfected maggots are introduced into the wounds where they feed on necrotic tissue thereby clearing debris from the area. Thus they have been used in many medical centers around the Western world. Maggots are also attracted to the rotting tissues of dead bodies that are left exposed to the environment. This has been dramatized in horror movies and television shows. The film Phenomena *starring Jennifer Connelly (1985) has a scene containing a swimming pool full of rotting corpses and maggots. The decay of human tissues at ambient temperatures attracts flies within 24 hours of death. This fact is used by some medical examiners and coroners to estimate the time*

This story is similar to a recent trend that is c

middle and early high school students. Based on videos posted on You-Tube, children are snorting candies labeled "Smarties." The candy is crushed into a fine powder and snorted up nasal cavities. Unlike many recreational drugs, this practice, while not illegal, is also not known to produce euphoria or elation. Therefore it is unclear why pre-teenagers would do this except to be rebellious. Unfortunately, there have been reports of small flies attracted to the sugar contained in these candies, and lay larvae eggs inside their noses. Given that houseflies feed on animal and human waste materials, these children, as well as the homeless man in this story are exposing their nasal cavities to fecal matter. Besides the disgusting thought of inhaling fecal vapors, there can also be transmission of microbiological diseases that are contained within stools. Individuals have also reported flies laying eggs into their ears, resulting in maggot infestation. The symptoms include feeling a wriggling sensation and scratching noises. Fortunately, these cannot travel from the ear canal into the brain, or out the other ear.

Gone Batty

Hank was the youngest of three siblings. His twin brother and sister were 12 years older than Hank. Hank's mother was 38 years old when Hank was born. During her pregnancy, cytogenetic analysis revealed that her fetus was male and had three copies of chromosome 21. Nevertheless, she proceeded to full term and delivered Hank, who developed Down's syndrome. Hank was a happy child and went to a special school. He was not as mentally challenged as many of his classmates. Hank was engaging and inquisitive. Hank loved animals, and at home, he had a Siamese cat and a German Shepard as pets. He did not mind cleaning the litter box and loved walking his dog.

Hank's father was a missionary for the church. When Hank was 12, he and his family relocated to Monrovia, the capital city of Liberia. His father would go into the villages on the outskirts of town while he and his mother stayed in an apartment in town. Hank went to an English-speaking school in Monrovia. One day, Hank and the rest of his classmates went on a field trip to the zoo. His teachers paired off each pupil with another and were told to stay together as a group. Hank and another boy, Alfred, were assigned together. They were visiting the elephant exhibit when Hank suggested that they split off from the others.

"Let's go to the bat house," he told Alfred.

"No Hank, Mrs. Okrodudu said we had to stay together."

"Elephants are boring. I want to see the bats. Come on, lets go!" was Hank's reply.

Alfred and Hank broke away from the others when their teacher wasn't looking and went to the bat pavilion. There, Hank was fascinated by the bats that were asleep and hanging upside down by their hind legs. Hank tried to get the attention of one bat. There were fruits and nuts on the ground but the bat did not appear to be hungry. Hank tried to entice the flying mammal to eat, so he picked up an apple off the ground and pretended to eat it.

"Look batman. Hmmm, yummy. Real gooood." But the bat ignored the child. Maybe if he heard me take a bite, the bat would awaken and be stimulated to eat, Hank thought. So he took a big bite, which created a loud crunching noise, and then Hank started chewing. Hank did not realize that the bat had already taken a small bite from that same apple and had discarded it. Alfred was horrified at seeing Hank eating the half-eaten discarded apple.

"What are you doing? You're going to get into real trouble when I tell the teacher" he said.

"Don't be a tattle tale," Hank said to the boy. Alfred ran out of the bat house to be with the other pupils. Hank tossed the apple back onto the ground where he found it and left the pavilion to join the others. No one knew the pair had gone astray.

*

Our hospital sees a lot of patients with a history of foreign travel. There are many people from our city who work as doctors, missionaries, reporters and scientists in Africa. We took the news of the latest Ebola virus outbreak with more than just a passive interest. When two Americans returned to the U.S. from West Africa because of Ebola infections, the news from Liberia became real to us. Dr. Kastle, the head of the clinical laboratory gathered his section chiefs and senior supervisors for a meeting.

"How is Ebola transmitted?" I asked our Dr. Helman, our microbiologist and local expert on the subject.

"Ebola is transmitted through direct contact with blood or bodily fluids from an infected animal or individual," he said. "It does not appear to be transmitted through the air."

"What protective equipment should we be wearing?" one of the senior supervisors wanted to know.

Dr. Helman responded. "The CDC has issued guidance for handling specimens for patients suspected of an Ebola virus infection." We all knew that CDC meant the Centers for Disease Control and Prevention in Atlanta. "I have ordered special water-resistant gowns. Our techs should wear two pairs of gloves when working with specimens. They must also wear foot covers, full face shields, and N95 masks to cover their nose and mouth." These masks have been approved by the FDA and CDC for Ebola virus protection.

"How do we determine that Ebola is present in the first place?" I asked, knowing that we have never seen a case and we don't have a diagnostic laboratory test available.

Dr. Kastle responded. "The CDC offers a test using reverse transcriptase-PCR." This is a molecular test that detects the specific RNA sequences known to be associated with the virus. "Detecting specific antibodies to the virus is also performed by the CDC, although this may not be positive during the early stages of the disease."

"We need to discuss these precautions with the lab," Dr. Kastle said. He adjourned the meeting and scheduled a series of open meetings with the technical staff. Dr. Kastle described a lab-wide safety plan, should we encounter an Ebola case. Most of our technologists thought that the precautions we suggested were reasonable.

One of the senior techs responded. "We have been through this before. When the AIDs epidemic first hit, we didn't know what we were dealing with." That was true. There were no treatments and a lot of people died in the U.S. during the first few years of this outbreak.

Another tech said, "We already exercise the concept of 'standard precautions'. According to the U.S. Occupational Safety and Health Administration, the clinical laboratory should "treat all human blood and certain human body fluids as if they were known to be infectious for HIV, HBV and other blood borne pathogens."

But Oscar, one of the younger techs responded. "That may be fine with you, but I am uncomfortable with this attitude of "business as usual." He pulled out a copy of the CDC HIV Surveillance report from 2009. "There have been at least 57 documented cases of occupational HIV transmission to healthcare workers. I think we need to do more to protect ourselves."

I could see that many of the other techs agreed with this

stance.

"What do you suggest?" Dr. Kastle asked.

Oscar responded. "Maybe we just don't offer clinical laboratory testing. The doctors can treat them as if they have Ebola based on a presumptive diagnosis." The tech was right, there are no Ebola virus-specific drugs. Treatment involves supportive care such as balancing fluids and electrolytes and administration of blood thinners. Unlike hepatitis B, there are no vaccines that can be taken to protect the staff. "Why should we risk our lives?"

Dr. Kastle was beginning to get concerned by this discussion because he sensed that others were agreeing with Oscar through their body language. He felt he had to reiterate the mission of the hospital and our lab. "Your points are valid. We do need to take every possible precaution to protect our staff. Nevertheless, to not perform any laboratory tests on such patients is not an option. We are a hospital. Our job is to provide the best medical care possible. You knew the risks when you chose this profession. It is not time to back out now. I hope nobody shirks their responsibility. What if the patient is one of your loved ones? You would expect the very best from us."

After an uncomfortable period of silence, I spoke up. "Maybe there is a middle ground."

"What do you mean?" Dr. Kastle asked me. I could see that he appreciated me breaking up the tension in the conference room.

"What about using our point-of-care testing devices?" These are convenient handheld laboratory tests that we use in the emergency room, operating room, and intensive care units.

Testing is done at the bedside by caregivers. Since samples do not need to be transported to the lab, this testing reduces the time required to report a result. Producing a result quickly for tests such as blood gases and electrolytes can have a positive impact on the care of critically ill patients. We also make these devices available in case of natural disasters. If there is a power outage such as an earthquake, we can use these battery-powered instruments at any time. In preparation for this possibility, we keep reagents on hand for emergency use.

"A major advantage of using portable testing devices is that they operate on whole blood." The techs knew that the centrifugation step, which itself can cause some release of aerosols from the sample, is eliminated. "If we have patients suspected of an Ebola infection, we can designate one of the testing devices to be used on these patients' blood and conduct the test under our biosafety hood," I concluded.

"But doesn't working with Ebola require a level 4 biosafety laboratory?" Oscar asked.

"That is true if you are doing experiments directly with the virus. We are only trying to contain the microorganisms while we conduct basic clinical laboratory analysis" Dr. Helman explained. "There are only a few level 4 biosafety labs in the U.S., yet every hospital has the potential to see a patient infected with Ebola."

"We don't have a point-of-care device for hematology," Oscar said. "And we can't put this instrument under the hood." Oscar worked in our chemistry laboratory where samples are uncapped and delivered by track to the testing equipment. His concern was aerosolization and splashing of serum during the transport process. The hematology director spoke up. "We don't have to remove the cap for any of our hematology analyzers. There is a probe that pierces through the rubber stopper and aspirates blood directly from the original blood collection tube. There is little or no opportunity for blood exposure."

"I wish our chemistry analyzer did that," Oscar said to me.

I have often wondered why chemistry manufacturers don't offer this feature. It would certainly be an initial marketing advantage over the competition. Over the years, I have also wondered why hematology analyzers move samples from right to left, while chemistry instruments move in the opposite direction. I guess it's like jacket zippers where the slider is on the right for men and left for women, I thought to myself. I stopped daydreaming and focused my attention back to the discussion at hand.

"We will need to validate the chemistry assays on our point-of-care devices," Dr. Kastle said directly to me. While we use the devices for measuring sodium and potassium, we have not used these instruments for blood gases.

"It will be expensive, because the reagents outdate after a few months. We will have to discard them and restock the supply on a periodic basis," I stated. "We might spend a lot of money in preparation for something that we hope may never happen."

"I understand that this is the price we might have to pay," Dr. Kastle remarked. I think this is a good alternative for providing laboratory care while protecting our staff as much as possible.

I then asked, "what about blood transfusions? Can we

dispense with the risk of typing and give everyone type O negative?"

"This could be considered, recognizing that there are risks to the recipient even with the use of O negative," Dr. Kastle remarked.

Then the discussion turned towards disposal of specimens and contaminated personal protective clothing. We all agreed that they must be carefully incinerated or immediately autoclaved. This would ensure that nobody accidently gets exposed. After the meeting, I was assigned the task of validating the point-of-care tests prior to making them available in an emergency.

"Finally, it might be helpful if we designated certain individuals from each lab to take the lead in handling these cases. We would provide special training and rehearse the procedures that may be needed." I stated. "A similar approach was taken at Emory University where several of patients exposed to Ebola from West Africa were taken. Are there any volunteers?"

"I volunteer to be one of those people," Oscar said proudly.

*

Hank felt sick about 3 days after his visit to the zoo. He had a fever, abdominal pain, vomiting and diarrhea. A few weeks earlier, the first cases of the 2014 Ebola epidemic occurred in Monrovia. Because Hank was at the zoo and was mentally challenged, public health officials interviewed his teachers and Hank's classmates. They checked the list and saw that Hank was paired up with Alfred. After being convinced that it was in Hank's best interest, Alfred told the investigators that he saw Hank take a bite out of an apple that he found lying on the ground near the bat cage. Alfred thought nothing of it but the investigators were secretly horrified. They hid this from the young boy in order to not alarm him unnecessarily.

"Are we in trouble?" he asked.

"No, everything is going to be fine," the school principal said.

The team of investigators went to the zoo and investigated the exhibit. The bat exhibit was in disrepair and there was a hole whereby neighbouring fruit bats had access to food at night. All of the bats were tranquilized and blood was taken–to test for the presence of Ebola virus. Several of them tested positive, so all of the bats were destroyed. The pavilion was closed pending a thorough decontamination and repair of the facility. Oscar was transported to Emory University Hospital in Atlanta. Unfortunately, his infection had progressed too far, and he became the first American to die of an Ebola infection.

*

As of this writing, there have been no Ebola virus deaths among Americans in the U.S. This story highlights one of the possible routes of transmission of the virus. Fruit bats are thought to carry the virus and infect other animals. Consuming bushmeat from infected animals can also cause the transmission of Ebola. Bush meat has been loosely defined as meat from wild African, Asian or South American animals. This practice has led to reduced numbers of some species to the point of near extinction. There have been international efforts to ban the practice of hunting wild animals for their meat, especially apes and gorillas. However, enforcing these laws is difficult to achieve out in the wilderness.

Ebola is transmitted from one human to another through direct contract of body fluids (e.g., blood, urine, semen) containing the virus.

The incubation phase, before the subject has any symptoms, lasts between 2 and 21 days. Fortunately, this individual is not infectious to others. After treatment, the patient may still be infectious for up to a week.

A viral glycoprotein is produced which alters the host immune defense. The protein also interferes with the ability of the host to recognize the virus as foreign. Human infections cause a defect in the ability of the host to clot. As a result, bleeding occurs at different sites. Death occurs within 1 to two weeks after the first appearance of symptoms. The mortality rate has been estimated to be between 50 and 90%. Treatment is currently supportive. There is no cure although the FDA has allowed the use of experimental RNA interference drugs. There has been some success in the development of a vaccine in primates. However, immunization requires 6 months and is of no use in an acute infection. Work is underway to develop a faster acting vaccine.

Most people don't recognize that health care can be a very high risk occupation. This is particularly true for doctors, nurses, respiratory therapists, phlebotomists, physician assistants, etc., who care for patients with infectious diseases. The clinical laboratory is also vulnerable as they must work with infectious body fluids such as blood and urine. Just like an FBI agent who wears bullet-proof vests, laboratory technologists must don personal protective equipment. But unlike law enforcement where a shooting is an overt event, transmission of a microbe is a covert event. An infection might not be evident for many days or even weeks after it occurs. So, one might not even know that they have been compromised. In this regard, our laboratory techs are just as courageous as police officers except that their stories are not documented in the press, or dramatized in cinema.

Wanderer

They came from all walks of life. Some of them were successful businessmen in their prior lives and gave up six-figure incomes to live there. Some came for health reasons. The fresh mountain and forest air cleansed their bodies from societies' modern pollutants. Others were there because they were hiding something from a checkered past. A failed marriage. A tragedy in the family. Perhaps some committed a crime and needed a safe haven from the authorities. Almost everyone lived there because they desired to have a simpler life. One that was devoid of the stresses of their former existence. There were no cell phones, computers, internet, television, radio, newspapers, or electronics of any kind. Everybody had equal status within the community. All had jobs to do. As much as possible, they grew and ate their own vegetables. "We have practiced organic farming years before it became fashionable elsewhere," many have said. Residents also raised farm animals for their food supply. The community was near a mountain spring which provided a largely unlimited supply of fresh water. Fish were caught from these waters and consumed. Some artistically talented members produced arts, crafts, and toys, which were sold to outsiders. Modern and traditional art figures were sculpted out of wood. Some produced rustic furniture. Others produced toys, dolls, and decorative kites. The money raised from these activities was pooled and used to buy tools, building and farm equipment, and school supplies.

All of the adults took responsibility for raising the children. Parents took turns teaching the children in their school. In addition to the usual reading, writing, and math, the emphasis was placed on nature and their surroundings. Ecology and conservation were also taught. There was plenty of opportunity for physical education. During the summer months, clothing was optional for both the children and adults although this was not a nudist colony. Imperfect as they were, they felt no shame in exposing their bodies. They lived all together in one community. This was the Fruitvale Commune.

*

Mars and Tulip were born and lived their entire life at Fruitvale. Their parents discarded their last names as they were unnecessary at the Commune. Mars' parents were among the "Founding Fathers" of the Community, formed shortly after the Woodstock Festival in New York. There were no formal marriages at Fruitvale, couples came together and broke up, just like conventional families. Mars and Tulip are the same age and were inseparable while they were growing up. They were somewhat unique in the commune in that they were strictly monogamists. Tulip gave birth to their child while they both were in their early thirties. Fruitvale had mid-wives that helped mothers deliver their children without need for hospitals, doctors, or anesthetics. When the baby arrived, it was a boy. The couple named him "Wanderer."

During his childhood, Wanderer became true to his namesake. At 10 years old, it would not be uncommon for him to run off into the woods with other children or be alone for hours at a time. The Fruitvale Commune was fairly remote, and as such, was largely safe. There were no reports of any serious crimes or child abductions. Tulip and Mars left Wanderer alone to find and commune with nature. One day when he was in his early teenage years, Tulip noticed an insect was attached to his upper inner thigh between his legs next to his scrotum. He was foraging for wild berries at the time. Wanderer felt no pain or discomfort. He only noticed because he was naked and the black bug stood out against his white skin. He took his finger and squeezed the critter dead before removing it. Later he felt bad that he was so cruel to one of God's creatures.

Within a few days, a rash form onto Wanderer's skin. It was not an unusual sight for Wanderer, because he was often brushed against poison ivy, oak, and sumac while in the woods. He also had his share of insect bites. But this rash was unusual. It had a red inner circle in the middle where he had been bit. There was a second peripheral red ring surrounding the inner circle. The pattern looked like a bull's eye. When he returned to his home, he showed it to one of the older boys who joked, "Did you get that at Target?" The comment was made because the rash looked just like the department store's logo. Wanderer had never been to town so he didn't catch the meaning of the remark.

A few days later, Wanderer noticed significant swelling of his scrotum. At first, he hid this from his parents by wearing a loin cloth. His parents didn't comment on this change in his behavior. But later, he began experiencing flu-like symptoms. He had a fever, chills, and his body ached all over. He took a turn for the worse and was bed-ridden for several days. Prior to this, Wanderer was extremely healthy. Members of the Commune remarked that living in the country made them hardy. Wanderer heard from his parents that, "the absence of chemicals and contaminants makes us strong." This statement was hypocritical because many in the Commune regularly smoked cigarettes and marijuana grown from their own farms, and exposed their members to second and third-hand smoke. The good health among residents may have been due to non-sterile living conditions which exposed residents to a variety of natural antigens causing them to have a heightened immune system.

Wanderer's medical condition worsened in the ensuing months. He developed neurologic symptoms that began to impair his motor function. There was no doctor living in the community. One of the women practiced nursing prior to joining the Commune and was the resident medical expert. She told Wanderer to drink plenty of water and to rest in bed. He was given homemade chicken soup, and told to wear a garlic necklace. But none of these measures helped Wanderer's medical condition. He developed paralysis on the left side of his face resulting from the dysfunction of one of his cranial nerves. At that point, Wanderer's parents felt it was time to seek the help of a western doctor. Wanderer arrived at the local hospital nearest to the Fruitvale Commune and was admitted under a diagnosis of "fever of unknown origin."

Dr. William Branford was a general practice pediatrician who saw Wanderer. He and some of his medical staff gathered around Wanderer's bed to discuss his case. One of them asked

Dr. Branford why Wanderer appeared to have Bell's Palsy.

"Bell's Palsy can be caused by a variety of diverse etiologies," Dr. Branford told them. "It can be caused by diabetes, stroke, brain tumor, or head trauma. A CT scan of the head was negative for a tumor or a bleed. Given that none of the other etiologies are evident from the history taken from the patient and his parents, we need to look for an infectious disease etiology. The important infections that can produce Bell 's Palsy are herpes zoster, viral meningitis, Lyme disease, and to a lesser extent, human immunodeficiency virus. I did a thorough examination of Mr. Wanderer's body, oral cavity, and genitals and found no lesions. I also inquired if he had any insect bites but he denied having any. Our working diagnosis is now meningitis. He lives in communal housing with a lot of close contact with other residents. We'll send blood to the lab for the necessary serologic tests."

Blood was sent to the laboratory for detection of antibodies directed towards a variety of infectious diseases including herpes, HIV, hepatitis A, B, and C, and Lyme disease. Blood was also cultured for the presence of bacteria. All of these tests came out negative. A lumbar puncture was performed by the careful insertion of a long needle directly into Wanderer's spinal cord. A small amount of cerebrospinal fluid was removed and sent to the laboratory for glucose and protein analysis, and cultured to detect the presence of bacterial meningitis. All of these results came out normal as well. Dr. Bransford was baffled. "We ordered a shot gun of tests that could have caused this and came up empty. Maybe he just had an influenza infection." Wanderer was treated with flu medications including an analgesic, antihistamine, and a decongestant.

The partial paralysis of Wanderer face resolved in the ensuing few days, and he was discharged from the hospital into the custody of his parents. Wanderer felt better but it didn't last. About a month after his hospital discharge, he developed worsening neurologic symptoms. This time, he was brought to the General Hospital where an infectious disease specialist was consulted. Dr. Chip Bass reviewed the boy's previous medical history and lab results from the other hospital, and did a thorough physical examination of Wanderer. He saw a reddened area on his thigh and questioned Wanderer about it. Although the boy originally denied any insect bites, this time he disclosed that he was bitten on the leg.

"Why didn't you tell the other doctors about this the first time you were seen?" Dr. Bass asked.

"I was walking through the woods naked at the time. The bite was high up on my leg. The people in my village warned me not to disclosure our nudity to strangers, because it is not accepted in your society."

Dr. Bass took some blood samples and sent them off to our laboratory at the General. Knowing that the traditional antibody tests were negative for all of the common viruses, this time, Dr. Bass requested for an additional analysis known as a western blot. This is a test that examines blood for the presence of specific antibodies directed against bacterial proteins. A polymerase chain reaction or PCR test was also ordered, a complementary procedure to the western blot. It is a test for the presence of DNA fragments from the virus itself. The PCR test was negative indicating either that there were no viral infections or that the virus particles were no longer in his system. However, the western blot showed the presence of antibodies that Wanderer's body developed to combat his infection. Together with the symptoms, this established the diagnosis. With this report, Dr. Bass told Wanderer that he had chronic stage 3 Lyme disease. He was treated with the appropriate antibiotics including doxycycline and amoxicillin, and sent home to Fruitvale. Dr. Bass thought, *he should have been diagnosed and treated with these drugs when he was seen the first time around.*

Wanderer suffered from his Lyme disease infection for many years to come. His joints would periodically ache limiting much of his physical activity. At the age of 15, he was prescribed medications to treat rheumatoid arthritis. His walks in the woods became increasing infrequent. Wanderer also complained of headaches and sleep problems. Tulip noticed that Wanderer, who was very content as a child, now had dramatic mood swings. As the result of his medical problems, Tulip pampered Wanderer as this was her only child. Mars, however, felt that the boy could take care of himself. The couple regularly argued over this and it eventually led to their separation. Mars hooked up with a woman 10 years his junior. When Wanderer reached the age of 21, he left Fruitvale. Tulip was devastated by his departure. He tried to enlist in the army but he failed his physical exam. So he took a job in town as a grade school teaching assistant. In order to not frighten the children, Wanderer legally changed his first name to Perry, Latin for traveler, and his last name to Cain, who was exiled after he killed his brother. Perry Cain felt he was exiled from the life and health he knew as a child.

*

In the United States, Lyme disease is caused by an infection of *Borrelia burgdorferi*, named after Dr. Willy Burgdorfer, who was first to identify the bacteria. Lyme disease itself is named after the towns of Lyme and Old Lyme, Connecticut where the first cases were identified in 1975. The connection between deer ticks and Lyme disease was made in 1981. I was a postdoctoral fellow in the clinical chemistry laboratory in Hartford Hospital when the first cases occurred. A decade later, we saw many more cases. Even some of my colleagues in the lab contracted the infection.

The incidence of this infection in the Northeast and along the Atlantic coast of the U.S. ranges from 40 to 80 cases per 100,000. Lyme disease has spread west to other parts of the country, including a substantial infestation in California, and worldwide, particularly Europe and Asia, where the *B. afzelii* and *B. garinii* species are more prevalent. Given the problems of diagnosis such as the absence of an effective blood test for screening purposes, estimates are that the true incidence of Lyme disease is 10 fold higher than what is currently reported. Fortunately, death from Lyme disease is rather rare.

Borrelia is transmitted to humans via a bite of an infected deer tick carrying *Borrelia*. The tick's nymphal stage is the most infectious. These ticks are hard to visualize and localize because they are about the size of a poppy seed. In about 80% of cases, a rash forms at the site of the tick bite. When present, the rash resembles a bull's eye target. Rashes, however, can appear on other parts of the body. Lyme disease can be successfully treated with antibiotics, if given during the early phase of the infection. Left untreated as in Wanderer's case, chronic symptoms can persist for many years. There are currently no vaccines available.

The current serologic test for Lyme disease is inconsistent, with a sensitivity of 50-60%, or slightly better than a coin flip. Falsely negative results can occur if blood is tested before antibodies develop or if treated early, there may be no antibody production. *Borrelia* is very difficult to culture in the laboratory, excluding this as an option. Currently, the most effective laboratory test to confirm the diagnosis of Lyme disease is the use of the western blot or PCR, although the performance of the test is dependent on the stage of the disease and type of specimen tested. Tests can also be conducted on the ticks themselves to determine if the offending insect is infected with *Borrelia*. Wanderer did not keep the tick that infected him, therefore none was available for testing. The Fruitvale Community denied a request by the Department of Public Health to visit their property looking for deer ticks infected with *Borrelia*. A search of the surrounding area came up negative for infected ticks. The Department issued warnings to the Fruitvale residents regarding Lyme disease.

Because the laboratory test used initially on Wanderer produced a falsely negative result, his illness was misdiagnosed and inappropriately treated. When the proper antibiotics were given, his disease had progressed, and Wanderer suffered more serious effects from the infection than was necessary. A lesson that Wanderer found out the hard way is to never go foraging through the woods naked

Wet Mount

Carla completed her clinical laboratory scientist or CLS training in Kansas City, Missouri. A few months before her graduation, her husband took a job at a start-up company in the Silicon Valley. They were thrilled to move to the West Coast where the temperatures are moderate and the mosquitoes are minimal. Carla found out from her internship at a private Kansas City hospital that the microbiology laboratory was her preferred specialty. When she received her California CLS license, we hired her in the microbiology lab at the General Hospital.

Carla was trained on all of the benches in the lab. Although she had experience with most of the techniques from her internship, the scope of testing and the medical microbiology problems that are seen in California are different from those seen in the Midwest. Towards the end of her training program, Carla was assigned to the "ova, cyst, and parasite" bench. These tests involve the examination of stool specimens for parasites that infect the intestinal tract.

"Back in Kansas City, we rarely saw any positive results," Carla remarked to Clancy, who was assigned to teach her that day. Clancy had worked in our lab for over 20 years and had seen it all. "We don't have a lot of travelers from third world countries," Carla said to Clancy. Carla knew that parasitic infestations occurred in overcrowded living conditions with poor sanitation. *Wait until you see what I have for you,* was Clancy's thought.

Consuela was instructed to go to the back of the lab where stool specimens are kept. She retrieved samples that had been tested that week. There were three specimens, stored at room temperature, that were taken from the same patient on consecutive days. Consuela asked Carla to examine the specimens visually and prepare a wet mount for each of the specimens according to the lab's operating procedures, and to examine them under the light microscope. This was a test of Carla's training and lab interpretation skills.

Carla put on her laboratory coat, apron, gloves, and googles and took the specimens from Clancy and walked over to the microbiology specimen hood. Each stool sample was in a large container that looked like paint can. Carla carefully opened the can and visually examined the specimen. The feces contained loose particles in a watery matrix. Carla was not exposed to the odors coming from the specimen, as the smell was directed into the biosafety hood and out the exhaust. Testing feces can be unpleasant and it is not for everyone. But Carla knew this was important work and she did not shy away from the exercise. Clancy was impressed with Carla's eagerness and professional approach.

Carla took out a bottle of saline and with an eyedropper, put a drop of the liquid onto a microscope cover slide. She then took a clean swab and wiped the stool specimen and mixed it with the saline on the glass slide. Carla then placed the slide onto the stage of the two-headed microscope, turned on the stage light, and then looked at the image under 10x low magnification and then at 40x power. Using the focus knob, she brought the specimen into sharp view. She moved the slide left and right, and up and down hoping to see something significant. Clancy was standing behind Carla watching her student. Carla thought *there must be something here or she wouldn't be standing right behind me.* Satisfied that there was nothing on that slide, Carla put the first slide aside, and took out another clean slide from the box. The fact that the first specimen was negative does not rule out a positive result in one of the next two specimens. After 20 minutes of finding nothing, Carla retrieved the second day's specimen and repeated the testing process. Again after another 20 minutes of examination, she again saw nothing. Now she retrieved the third of the three specimens and prepared the wet mount. By now some of the other techs, who knew the exercise that Clancy had planned, were looking at Carla from their seats. Perseverance is a sign of a good clinical lab scientist particularly a microbiologist.

Carla thought that at some point, she will have to conclude that the specimen is devoid of any pathogenic material. Carla was about to stop when she finally saw IT. She couldn't believe her eyes. She had never seen IT before during her training. She had only seen IT in textbooks. She moved the slide back and forth while looking under the microscope, to view IT at every angle. IT was alive and moving slowly! She switched the stage lens to the 40x high power magnification to get a better view. She couldn't take her eyes away from the scope. Nothing else entered her mind in those few minutes. She got a twinge in her back having sat slumped over the scope for those minutes, but it didn't stop her examination. When she was finally finished, she sat back in her chair and said "Oh, wow" while still looking down. Then she looked up and saw that most of the other lab techs had stopped what they were doing and had gathered around her bench. They were all quietly watching her. Perhaps they too had these feelings the first time they saw IT. Carla did not hear them coming and as she looked around, she was surprised at their presence. Clancy slowly clapped her hands together, which led the others to follow suit. I was in my office next door and stuck my head out to see what the commotion was all about. Carla was embarrassed by all of the attention. Her face turned red. But she knew then and there that she passed the test and would become one of them. Carla could not wait to tell her husband what she found. While he was happy for her success, he didn't want to hear too much of the "messy" details. Such is the life of a clinical microbiologist.

*

Rahul and Janet were both majoring in social work in college and met as freshmen. Rahul had strong feelings for Janet and was hoping that they could be a couple. Janet wanted to maintain a platonic and not a romantic relationship. Rahul was content to be her friend and classmate.

The department's curriculum offered a "study abroad" elective whereby students could get credit while working as a counselor in a third world country. The school had established relationships with several countries in Africa and Southeast Asia. During the spring semester of her junior year, Janet signed up for the exchange program in a small village in the Philippines.

Their assignment was to learn about the culture, and work with village school children and their teachers.   When Rahul found out that Janet was headed to that program, he too enrolled hoping to get closer to Janet. Maybe it was because he was the only one of her age around. Or it could have been that she found comfort from someone that she already knew while she was in a very foreign country. Whatever the reason, Rahul's plan worked. Within a few weeks of their arrival on the island, Janet gradually became more attached to Rahul.   From a friendship, this blossomed into a romance. During their off time, they went on walks together, holding hands and kissing when no one was watching. Two days before the end of the program, Rahul made his move. *It's now or never*, he said to himself. They had a free afternoon and Rahul suggested that they go swimming in a river that they had discovered during one of their walks.

"I didn't bring any bathing suits," Janet said.

"Me neither," Rahul said. "But there is nobody around. We can go skinny dipping."   They grabbed some towels and headed for the river.

When they got there, Janet said to Rahul as she was removing her clothes, "turn your back around please. No peeking."

Rahul reluctantly agreed. Janet disrobed and went into the warm water. Rahul jumped in a minute later, feet together, knees to his chest, making a big splash. The two frolicked in the water for the better part of an hour.   What they didn't know was that upstream, the villagers were using the river as their main route for disposal of human waste. When the two climbed out of the river, they felt clean and refreshed.   They returned to the village, took a shower, and made love for the first time. Rahul had brought condoms hoping this day would arrive.

At the end of the week, the program was over and Rahul flew back to the U.S. It was their summer break. Rahul had a summer job in a research lab on campus. A routine medical check was conducted on his return. Rahul reported no medical complaints and was issued a clean bill of health.

Janet arranged to stay an additional 3 months in the Philippines. She landed a job as an English language tutor to grammar school students. Four weeks after Rahul left, Jane developed severe abdominal pain. She could not stand and was doubled over in pain. This was followed by bloody and watery diarrhea. The villagers thought she had food poisoning and that her symptoms would pass with rest. But her symptoms did not subside. She was sent to Manila where doctors suspected a parasitic infection. She was treated with metronidazole, an antibiotic used to treat some parasitic infections. When she was stable, she was put on a plane back to the U.S.

Janet had a note from the Filipino doctors that she was suffering from a gastrointestinal disease, but it was not an airborne illness therefore she was deemed not to be contagious. The airline gave her a seat next to the plane's bathroom. It was a long and arduous trip, as Janet spent a large amount of time moaning and groaning while on the toilet. Fortunately, the noise of the airplane drowned her cries. Passengers seated next to her donned their noise-cancelling headphones and ignored her during the entire flight. When she reached the U.S., she was taken to the General Hospital.

Janet's stool samples were collected, one each day she

spent at the General. The clinical microbiology lab performed a microscopic analysis on Janet's feces. The report came back positive for trophozoite and cysts of the *Entamoeba histolytica*. Janet was seen by Dr. Harrison Schaudinn, an infectious disease specialist. He questioned her about how she might have gotten this infection.

"Did you drink water that might have been contaminated?" he asked her.

"We were trained to avoid consuming any untreated or un-boiled water. We received a lecture about traveler's diarrhea. The school provided us with bottled water. We avoided eating fresh fruits and vegetables because they could be cleaned with dirty water," Janet explained. "We were also told that poor hygiene can cause infections, so I was careful in my physical contacts with the villagers. I was there for several months and never had any problems."

"Montezuma's revenge is typically caused by a bacterial infection like *E. coli* or *Salmonella*," Dr. Schaudinn remarked, referring to Janet's comment about traveler's diarrhea. "You have a parasite. Did you do any swimming while you were there?" Dr. Schaudinn asked.

"There was this one time when my colleague, Rahul and I went swimming in a river. It looked clean so I didn't think anything about it. I have been in contact with him since his return and he reports no problems," Janet said." She didn't tell the doctor that they were naked in the water. Then a sudden horrible thought came to her mind. *Could I have been infected through the vaginal route?*

Dr. Schaudinn continued. "Amoeba infections occur

through oral exposure." This information gave her some relief that she wasn't infected through vaginal, urethral, or anal exposure. "The majority of amoeba infections are asymptomatic. They can remain dormant in the host for many years. It is possible that your friend is also infected and doesn't know it. Give the nurse his contact information at school and we will check with his doctor. It is possible that you accidently drank some of the river water?"

"Yes, when Rahul jumped in, and I remember some of the water ended up in my mouth," Janet disclosed.

"Many of the villages use rivers and streams for sewerage. This may have been the route of your infection."

"I am feeling much better now," Janet said. She had been in the hospital for the past few days. "When can I go home?"

"Because your diarrhea is bloody, we are concerned that you have ulcers in your intestines. If the amoeba entered your blood stream, you may other complications such as liver abscesses. We will do some follow-up tests to determine this," Dr. Schaudinn said.

Blood was taken from Janet and tested for antibodies to the infection. When the results came back positive, Dr. Schaudinn concluded that her infection had gone into her blood stream. An abdominal CT scan was performed which confirmed that she had liver abscesses, pus filled cavities. The abscess fluid was drained from her liver and she was treated with antibiotics.

"You are lucky you came home," Dr. Schaudinn said to her upon her discharge from the hospital after a week. "Liver abscesses are fatal if misdiagnosed and untreated."

Janet returned to school for her senior year. Rahul

tested negative for active parasites. He was told, however, that he may have dormant cysts and could become symptomatic many years later. While Janet never blamed Rahul for her infection, she broke off their relationship. She wanted to move on with her career and seeing Rahul made her think of an unpleasant end to her study abroad.

*

Amoebiasis is an infection caused by the amoeba Entamoeba histolytica. *Some 50 million people throughout the world are infected, mostly in warm climates. There are some 50,000 deaths each year. An individual with amoebiasis will produce cysts that are excreted into the feces. These cysts are stable for several months outside of the host and are capable of transmission to humans through oral ingestion, normally of contaminated water. Cysts are more stable in warm water. Once in the body, cysts undergo excystation, a process where trophozoites, the active form of the amoeba, are formed in the digestive tract. For most cases, the amoeba lives as a cooperative parasite, surviving by digesting food in the gut consumed by the person, without damaging host tissues and organs. Trophozoites form cysts via encystation, and are excreted into feces, thereby completing the amoeba's life-cycle. When trophozoites invade the intestinal mucosa, they release digestive enzymes that degrade cell membranes and proteins, allowing these organisms to enter into the circulation. While the liver is the most common target, injury to the brain, lungs, and spleen can also occur.*

The microbiology lab at the General was successful in detecting Entamoeba histolytical *in one of Janet's watery stool samples. They were also able to find dormant cysts present under the microscope. Carla received experience in seeing a positive result, something she would not soon forget. The serology test for amoeba antibodies was conducted in a* reference lab and not the microbiology laboratory because this infection is not common in the U.S. Molecular tests that detect amoeba DNA in feces are also now available but are not in widespread use.

Amoeba outbreaks are uncommon in the U.S. due to good hygiene practices. However, during the 1933 World's Fair in Chicago, there were 1000 cases with 58 deaths due to contamination of water from defective plumbing. Bad plumbing at the Oakland Coliseum where the Oakland A's and Raiders play their home games, led to fecal contamination of water in 2013. Fortunately nobody got sick.

.

Because She Was Not There

Marla Evans had been teaching in the same school district for over 30 years. She never married. Her mother had gotten sick soon after Marla graduated from college, and Marla stayed home and cared for her mother rather than placing her in a nursing home. When her mom passed away, Marla was in her late thirties. The opportunities for marriage had passed her by, so she decided to devote herself to teaching. Marla taught early elementary school children for eight years, but got tired of the "babysitting" aspect of teaching young children and wanted something more academically challenging. She went back to school at night to obtain a master's degree in biochemistry. Soon after, she was teaching chemistry to high school juniors and seniors.

Marla was particularly proud of the number of her former students that ended up becoming doctors. Many of them said to her later that it was her guidance and enthusiasm that had led them into the world of science and medicine. At Marla's invitation, a few of them came back to the high school during "Career Day" to tell her current students about what it was like to be a doctor. These visits helped stimulate her current students to consider medicine as a career.

One of her former students became a pathologist and brought in a dark, shriveled-up liver from a patient who had died of cirrhosis, to show the students. The patient had a long history of alcohol abuse. The kids were grossed out looking at the liver, which was part of Marla's intent. Another former student was a research scientist. He hosted students in his research laboratory during the summer so they could learn how to clone genes. A third former student became an oral maxillofacial surgeon. He traveled to Honduras for the Doctors Without Borders program and showed before and after pictures of children on whom the team had performed cleft lip reconstruction surgery.

*

During the winter break in January, Marla developed a recurrent cough. The hacking persisted over the better part of February. Since she wasn't getting better, she went to see her family doctor. She was asked to cough up several sputum samples into specimen cups. All of these mucous samples were clear. The cups were capped, sealed, and sent to the Rely Reference Laboratory for sputum culture testing for the presence of a particular type of organism called *Mycobacterium*. A chest x-ray was also conducted on Marla, and revealed no specific abnormalities. Marla told the doctor that she had no history of foreign travel to areas where tuberculosis was endemic.

A week later, the first of the sputum samples came back positive for *Mycobacterium tuberculosis*. This was despite the fact that Marla's other tests for tuberculosis, including the PPD skin test and a new test called quantiFERON, were negative. The laboratory was obligated to report the result to the Department of Public Health, or DPH, who sent an infectious disease nurse specialist to investigate Marla's apartment. The nurse did not find anything unusual. Nevertheless, the positive sputum culture findings reported to the DPH led their doctors to conclude that Marla had contracted tuberculosis, a highly infectious disease

The doctors told her that she needed to be quarantined so that she would not infect her students. She was treated with a cocktail of drugs consisting of isoniazid, rifampin, and pyrazinamide. The doctors told her that with treatment, she may be cleared to return to teach in a couple of months. In the meantime, she would have her sputum regularly collected and tested while she was in isolation. Marla was very upset with this news. She was rarely sick, and had never been away from work for more than a day or two. Now she was likely to miss the entire quarter. At first, Marla tried to keep up with her students by phone, email, and text messaging and giving extra reading assignments for extra credit. But most students ignored her requests. The school hired a temporary teacher, but he lacked Marla's drive and enthusiasm. Most of the students, even the better ones, lost interest in the subject. However, there was one student, Sunny, who maintained contact with Marla throughout her ordeal. Sunny was an Asian boy who at first was not that interested in chemistry, but as the school year went on, he became her best student. Thinking about her students and what they might become kept Marla sane during the awful weeks of isolation and helped her combat her general feelings of uselessness.

After the initial diagnosis was made and Marla was already in isolation for two months, a new infectious disease doctor, Dr. Louise Croft, came onto the case. She felt that something was not right about this case. There was only one positive sputum result for TB; all the other laboratory tests were negative. And although Marla's symptom of a persistent cough was consistent with TB, it also meant that she could have the flu. Her chest x-ray was negative and her sputum was clear, not green or bloody like that of a TB patient. So Dr. Croft contacted Rely Laboratories to investigate if the lab had made an error.

*

In order to understand how Marla's TB test went wrong, it is necessary to understand how errors occur. I used some of what happened in this case in a lecture I gave to my laboratory technology students regarding errors, and remembered a particular discussion with one of my students, Eunice.

"There are three types of lab errors," I told Eunice. "Most doctors are familiar with 'analytical' error. That is when a mistake is made during the testing process itself. Some examples might be an instrument malfunction, the presence of an interfering substance, or inaccuracies when it comes to measuring the amount of specimen to be taken from the blood sample. 'Post analytical error' occurs when there is a mistake made in the interpretation of test results."

"How frequent are errors made by doctors, Professor?" asked Eunice.

"In fact, Eunice, medical errors account for more than 100,000 deaths in the United States each year. After heart disease, it is the second leading cause of death. But most of these errors are not caused by mistakes in medications, nor are they the result of the inappropriate interpretation of laboratory tests."

"What is the third type of error?"

"That would be 'pre-analytical error,' a mistake made in where and how the sample was taken from the patient or what happens to it before it is tested."

"Can you give us an example of a pre-analytical error?" Eunice wanted to know.

"I was once asked to review laboratory procedures involving sputum culture testing for tuberculosis. The laboratory settled a lawsuit because they reported a false positive culture on a school teacher."

Eunice had heard about this case, but didn't know what had happened to cause the error.

"In preparing this specimen for culture, a chemical solution was added to sputum specimens and thoroughly mixed to liquefy the sputum," I continued. Once freed from the mucous proteins, the microorganisms can grow when placed on a culture medium. While the laboratory was processing a sample from the teacher, they were also liquefying samples from other patients at the same time. The tech unscrewed the caps of each sputum specimen and then added the digestion solution into each tube one at a time."

"I don't see why that would have caused a problem," Eunice said with a puzzled look.

"The process of adding the digestion solution and then shaking produces an aerosol of vapor from the samples," I explained. If these vapors contained microorganisms, they could have found their way into the next specimen, thereby contaminating it. The preferred technique is to open the cap of one tube at a time, add the solution, and then close the cap before opening the next sample. In the batch of samples, there were two positive results. The lab performed DNA analysis, which showed that the genetic signatures of both specimens were identical. The lab doing the test concluded that the contaminated specimen was from a school teacher who had no other positive sputum results, and no evidence of mycobacterium or clinical signs of a tuberculosis infection. This was discovered because of an alert infectious disease doctor who questioned the result and requested that the lab check its finding. In a written statement prepared for the treating doctor, the testing laboratory said that this cross-contamination had occurred, the result was a false positive, and while unfortunate, it was unavoidable."

"What recommendations did you make to this lab to improve their testing?" Eunice asked.

"I had the lab re-write their sample preparation procedure, which reduced the likelihood of this pre-analytical error ever occurring again. I redirected them to open one tube at a time, change pipette tips between specimens, and take other preventative measures against cross-contamination. I believe the lab no longer has experienced this as a problem."

"What happened to the teacher?"

"After it was confirmed that she didn't have tuberculosis, she went back to teach for the remainder of the school year. There was no apology from the testing laboratory. I don't believe they thought they had done anything wrong. Or maybe they were afraid of a negligence lawsuit since the teacher had to be quarantined. The teacher, in fact, never knew that she was not infected and that the need to isolate her had been unnecessary."

By my speaking tone, Eunice sensed that there might be

more to this story. "Did anything bad happen in her classroom while she was away?"

"Ah, well, yes something bad did happen," I said, reluctantly. Eunice was young and I didn't want to upset her unduly. But she asked, and besides, she needed to know the importance of what we do. "It actually was tragic. You see, there was this student of hers named Sunny...."

*

Sunny had emigrated with his family from Korea when he was four. Sunny's father died when he was 12; his mother was forced to get a job as a housemaid. She could not speak English and this was the best she could do. Sunny had twin sisters who were three years younger than he was. As the oldest, Sunny had to take care of his sisters after school and before his mother came home from her job. It was a difficult life for Sunny. There were many opportunities to get sidetracked. There was a local gang of Korean teenagers who tried hard to recruit Sunny into their group. They would bully him and steal his lunch money on occasion. Whenever he saw one of the gang members in school or on the street, Sunny would turn the other way or duck into an alley. He never told his mother that he was being harassed; he figured she had enough troubles just trying to make ends meet.

Sunny was an average student all through school. He was never really interested in any of the subjects. For him, school was largely about day-to-day survival. However, when he was a junior in high school, there was one class that stood out: chemistry, taught by Ms. Marla Evans. Ms. Evans made the class interesting and relevant. She told them why salt dissolves snow during the winter, and how an enzyme can break down food in their stomachs during digestion. Sunny felt that Ms. Evans took a genuine interest in him. None of his other teachers ever took the extra time that Ms. Evans did. At first, Sunny stayed after school to get extra help from Ms. Evans. By then, his sisters were old enough so that he didn't have to rush home to babysit them, and Marla was more than happy to help this interested student with his assignments. Besides, all she had waiting at home was her cat. But after a while, Sunny became comfortable with the class and didn't need the tutoring. Then Ms. Evans suggested that Sunny work on a project for the annual high school science fair. Sunny jumped at the idea. So with Ms. Evans' help, Sunny conceived of a chemistry project involving the dangers of third-hand cigarette smoke exposure. Unlike second hand smoke, where individuals are directly exposed to the smoke of a smoker, third-hand smoke related to exposures of toxins found in the environment of smokers, such as their clothing, furniture, walls, and floors. Using the school's liquid chromatograph, Sunny measured extracted nitrosamines from older apartments where smokers lived and compared the results to newer housing that was free of smokers. He worked with one of Marla's former students, who was a research scientist at a nearby college. At the school's science fair that was held in December, Sunny was awarded second place. He lost out to another student who cloned a gene linked to Alzheimer's disease. But his project and the other finalists were all selected for the citywide science fair competition. Marla was very proud of her pupil and believed that Sunny would be next in the long line of successful students whom she mentored.

The citywide science fair was scheduled for late March. Unfortunately, at that point in the school year, Marla Evans was on a leave of absence due to her alleged tuberculosis infect. Before she was forced into isolation, she'd promised to drive Sunny to the fair, which was at a downtown hotel. But that was no longer possible. It was a great disappointment to Marla that she couldn't be there for him.

On the morning of the science fair, Marla sent a text to her student. "Good luck, Sunny. I know you will make us all proud. I can't wait to see you again in person."

Sunny looked up the bus schedule and was waiting at the bus stop on the day of the fair. It was a Saturday morning. The competition was scheduled for 1:00 p.m. He had gotten a haircut and dressed up in his best clothes. His presentation was in the form of a large poster that was rolled up neatly into a tall cylindrical tube. He was alone at the stop waiting for the bus, when three of the Korean gang members spotted him.

"Hey Sunny boy, where are you going, all dressed up?" one of them asked.

"That's none of your business. Leave me alone," Sunny said, turning away to avoid making eye contact.

"What do we have there?" another one asked while eyeing the tube containing Sunny's science project. Then as Sunny was distracted by one, another gang member grabbed the tube.

"Give it back, I need it today," Sunny pleaded.

The boys started playing "keep away" with the tube, tossing it between themselves as Sunny tried to catch it. Sunny was getting irritated and fought back. He tackled one boy who had the poster, and they fell to the ground. The tube was flattened under the weight of their bodies. The two boys wrestled her for several minutes. The other two gang

d were yelling to encourage the fight.

..as getting the best of the bigger boy he was

..g. The other two boys started teasing their fellow gang member because he was losing this fight to the smaller boy; he had cuts in his lower lip from Sunny's fist, and was bleeding. Embarrassed, the bloodied boy pulled out a switchblade and stabbed Sunny once in the stomach. Sunny fell, hitting his head on the hard pavement. He was unconscious and bleeding profusely. Blood was seeping out of Sunny's body at a high rate. The poster that he was going to present later that day was soaked in his blood. The boys all ran, leaving Sunny lying on the ground, blood still seeping out.

A few minutes later, a pedestrian who saw the fight ran over to Sonny and immediately called 9-1-1 from his cellphone. An ambulance arrived, and Sunny was taken to the hospital. His major artery had been torn by the knife, and Sunny had lost a lot of blood. The hospital's massive blood transfusion protocol was quickly enacted. Because there was no time for blood typing and cross-matching, he was given type O blood. This was typical practice in an emergency. Despite a heroic effort by the emergency department staff, Sunny died while in the ER within a few hours of his arrival. The next day, the principal of the school was informed about what had happened by another student. He knew that Marla was close to Sunny so he called her. She was horrified and broke down crying. She felt utterly helpless sitting in her quarantined room. She couldn't even attend Sunny's funeral two days later because she was still in tuberculosis isolation. While it wasn't her fault, she blamed herself for

Sunny's death because she hadn't been there for him. If she hadn't been quarantined, she would have driven him to the science fair and everything would have been different. Marla would never forget Sunny and what his life could have been.

When the police canvassed the neighborhood, they found the witness who called and he was able to identify Sunny's assailants. The three Korean gang members were arrested and tried as adults. The boy who stabbed Sunny was convicted of second-degree murder and was sentenced to 25 years. The other two boys were convicted of being accomplices and were each sentenced to 10 years.

*

Microbiologic techniques for culturing the organism responsible for tuberculosis have improved over the years with automated culture testing equipment. The U.S. Centers for Disease Control has issued guidelines for the handling of specimens to minimize cross-contamination.

Even though I was initially reluctant to tell this story to my student because it was so sad, afterwards I was glad I had done so. She never forgot it and when she later joined our microbiology laboratory, she practiced with meticulous care.

Marla Evans' dedication to high school science students was an inspiration to me. She asked me to become a judge at the local science fair competitions. One of the high school students did a study in my laboratory during the summer and worked for me part- time while she was in college. She eventually became a medical technologist and works in my lab today.

Special Sauce

****

Nguyen Pham's father was a major in the South Vietnamese army. He was loyal to the corps and believed in the democratic freedom that his country was seeking from the Communist-ruled North Vietnam. He, his wife Nga and their infant son Cao were stationed in Saigon in 1975 during the fall of the city on April 30th. This led to the end of the "American War," as it was known in Vietnam at that time and even today by the Vietnamese. Nguyen instructed his wife and child to get on one of the last flights out of Saigon before the Communists took over the city, and suspended all airline and military operations. Nga pleaded with her husband to come with them to America.

"Gia đình của bạn cần bạn bây giờ hơn nước bạn. (Your family needs you now more than your country)" she said to Nguyen.

"Tôi có một nhiệm vụ để người đàn ông của tôi. Tôi không thể đi. Bạn sẽ được an toàn. Tôi đã sắp xếp cho một hộ tống đến Mỹ và thấy rằng bạn và những người khác đang định cư ở đó. Tôi sẽ tham gia cùng bạn càng sớm càng tốt. (I have a duty to my men. I cannot leave. You will be safe. I've arranged for an escort to America and to see that you and the others are settled there. I will join you as soon as possible)." Nguyen was actually thinking that he would not disgrace his family by retreating and not facing the enemy man-to-man.

Quietly, Nga was crying. It was a similar feeling to the time her parents were killed by a Viet Cong bomb in the city. She believed this would be the last time she would see her husband but there was nothing she could do to convince him otherwise. Nguyen at 35 was much older than Nga who was only 19 when she married him, just a few years ago. But she recognized that it was time for her to be strong for Cao's sake. She boarded the plane and held Cao tightly to her breast. Even though he was only 7 months old, he remained very quiet during the ordeal. It was as if he knew this was a turning point in their lives.

Major Nguyen Pham surrendered to the invading North Vietnam army. At first, they treated him with the respect that he deserved as a fellow officer. However, after he was stripped of his rank and uniform, he was sent to the Socialist Republic of Viet Nam's "Re-education" camp where he was tortured and forced to endure hard labor. The stated objective of the camp was to teach these former enemies the "ways of the government." Nguyen was forced to write confessions of his crimes and misdeeds. Many of his fellow officers and soldiers resisted and died in the camp from disease or starvation. Thinking of the day that he would reunite with Nga and Cao was the only thing that kept Nguyen alive. He realized that he should have left Saigon with his family on that last day.

*

Nga was given paperwork that allowed her to immigrate to the U.S. Many of the other refugees from Saigon were given

172

relocation "assignments." The legal authority for this immigration was granted under the Indochina Migration and Refugee Assistance Act, which was passed on May 23, 1975. Nga and other Vietnamese families were sent to Houston. These first waves of Vietnamese immigrants were from prominent families and were highly educated. Southeast Texas was selected because of its warm and humid climate, similar to Viet Nam. This area had a burgeoning economy due to the Oil Boom. Nga and Cao lived in a community of refugees, where she took a job as a cook. Cao stayed with some of the older members of the Vietnamese community.

Nga regularly contacted the Vietnamese Embassy hoping to find out what happened to her husband, but there was no word of his demise. Cao entered elementary school with no memory of his father. Life in Southeast Texas for the Vietnamese was very difficult during the early refugee years. The second and third waves of immigrants, also known as the "boat people" were from the working class. The fishermen took jobs working in the Gulf Coast shrimp industry. At first, they were welcomed as they did the dirty jobs that the residents didn't want to do. Later, local residents began to resent the refugees because as the Oil Boom of the late 1970s became the Oil Bust of the 1980s, many lost their jobs. Employers in the fishing industry preferred hiring Vietnamese workers because they did not complain, were illegally paid less, and many worked harder than some of their Caucasian counterparts. This resentment spilled into the local schools. Cao was smaller than the other children in his school and regularly bullied. Nevertheless, Cao was smart, studied hard, and maintained good grades.

Twelve years after they arrived in the U.S., Nga finally received word that her husband was alive and he had been released from a North Vietnam prison camp. It took another 6 months before the immigration paperwork was cleared by both countries. By 1988, Nguyen was on his way to Houston's Intercontinental Airport. Nga and Cao waited anxiously at the gate. Back then, you could go directly to the gate to meet passengers as the security was not as tight as it is today. When Nga saw Nguyen, she rushed to hug and kiss him. Cao stood behind and waited for his turn. The three hugged together for the first time in over a dozen years.

Nguyen had aged considerably while at the camp. He had lost all of his muscle tone and was a very thin gaunt man with prematurely gray and thinning hair. He also lacked the enthusiasm that he had when he was a young army officer. Nguyen had difficulty adjusting to American life. He lacked motivation. He would sit for hours alone in their small garden. It took him several months to find a job. Nguyen had nightmares about his time in prison and would wake up at night in a cold sweat. His captors had convinced him that he had no self-worth. Today, we would know this as post-traumatic stress disorder and there would be therapeutic options. For Nguyen, he had no medical options. Just about the time that Cao was ready to enter college, Nguyen died. His body and mind had given up. The Viet Cong had claimed yet another victim. Nga was alone again. But this time, she was really alone, as Cao went on to college in New York City on a full scholarship.

Cao listed biology as his major and excelled in his studies. He graduated *summa cum laude*. While in college, he met

Nancy Pho at the Vietnamese student club and they became close friends. Nancy's family immigrated to San Jose, California around the same time as Cao's family settled in Houston. She majored in finance and graduated a year ahead of Cao. Nancy earned a job at a major brokerage firm in the City and began dating Cao. Her office was on the 92nd floor of the World Trade Center's South Facade.

Cao graduated college a year later and enrolled in a graduate school in nearby Connecticut. He joined the research group of Felix Gooey, a noted veterinarian researcher in the pathobiology department. The school was only a few hours from Manhattan. Cao regularly visited Nancy. He hoped to marry her someday.

I met Cao because I was an adjunct faculty member in the department. Pathobiology ties together the science of biology, pathology, epidemiology and public health. Often, the experimental component for the human mechanism of disease is conducted on animal models. I joined this department because they were doing novel toxicological analyses. As an adjunct faculty, I helped supervise some students and sat on graduate student thesis committees for others. The department was small and I got to know many of the graduate students even if I wasn't supervising their thesis work.

Cao was in his second year of graduate school when he heard the news on his car radio as he was driving to school. Two commercial airplanes had crashed into the World Trade Center Towers, one in each tower. Cao ran into the building where his department was located and went straight to the break room where there was a television. The other students were gathered around the set watching the events unfold before their very eyes.

One of the students asked Cao, "don't you have a friend working at the World Trade Center?"

Cao didn't hear a word. He was already running out the door and back into his car, speeding towards New York. He wasn't sure what he was going to do when he got there. Cao tried to call Nancy on his cell phone but there was no response. He drove as far as the South Bronx. After that point, all of the roads were blocked off with only access by emergency vehicles. There was a mass of people leaving the city by foot. It was an orderly but heavily congested exodus. Cao left his car in a lot and went into the city against the pedestrian traffic. He was listening to latest news on his pocket radio and headset as he was walking. By then both towers and collapsed and he feared the worst for his girlfriend. It took hours for him to reach the outskirts of the area where the World Trade Center once stood. The air was thick with smoke which darkened the skies. A security team did not allow Cao to come near Ground Zero even after he told them that his friend was in the building. He was told that there was nothing he could do and they asked him to leave. Cao stayed on the street all night and into the next morning hoping for some news. He learned that the second plane hit the south tower between floors #77 and #85. Cao visited Nancy's office a few weeks earlier and knew she was on the 92nd floor. Cao drove back to campus and received confirmation a few days later that Nancy died in the attack. Her parents flew in for the memorial service. Cao took a leave of absence from the school and spent several months with his mother in Texas.

*

The next few months after the 9/11 attacks were among the darkest of days in American history. There were 23 attacks in the U.S. by anthrax between September and November, with 11 deaths by inhalation of this bacterium. Cao kept a close watch on the television at home. Anthrax was one of the pathogens that he was doing research on. He wondered if these attacks would affect his ability to conduct his research on West Nile virus.

Cao returned to campus in January of 2002. A few weeks later, the department received a letter from the U.S. State Department informing them that all forms of live anthrax had to be secured and registered with documentation as to the reason for retaining samples. Those deemed unnecessary must be destroyed. The Pathobiology Department Chairman forwarded the letter to each of their faculty members, graduate students and postdoctoral fellows. Cao was doing research on these bacteria and had 4 vials containing live anthrax cultures. The samples were collected during the late 1970s from an Anthrax-infected cow. Cao submitted three of the vials to the autoclave, an instrument that sterilizes and kills bacteria. However, he kept one vial in order to continue his work, and did not inform his mentor. He removed the vial from the general freezer from the department into his own research group's freezer.

An anonymous undergraduate student overheard Cao mention that he was using the anthrax strain as a reference for his studies, and contacted federal authorities. When the Feds arrived, they went on a search of the Pathobiology research lab. Within hours, the Pathobiology building was in a lockdown. All faculty, staff, and students were escorted to the school's auditorium and one by one, their credentials were checked.

Nobody was allowed to leave the premises. Anyone without a university identification card was held in a separate room and interrogated. Some students had forgotten to bring their ID card, a mistake they wouldn't make again. Others were visiting the campus with their parents. The FBI was looking in particular for the whereabouts of Mr. Cao Pham. Once Cao found out that he was the target of their search, he came forward and identified himself. He was immediately taken to another room where he was searched, cuffed, ushered into their police vehicle labeled with "SWAT", and driven away to their interrogation headquarters. This was all in plain sight of all of the students and faculty. Cao started weeping silently. He didn't know what was happening. He thought to himself that this is how his father might have felt when he was captured by the Viet Cong. He vowed to himself to be strong. A thorough background check was made on Cao. The FBI did a thorough examination of his dorm room. His computer and all research notebooks and files were confiscated.

A team dressed up in biohazard suits entered the laboratories and began a search of all refrigerators, freezers, benches, and shelves. Directed by Dr. Gouwei's postdoc, they went first to the locked freezer that contained Cao research samples. The entire contents of the freezer were removed and carefully inspected. The vial labeled as "anthrax" was put into a special vapor-locked container and sealed. It would be examined by qualified scientists at the FBI lab under a special bio hazardous laminar-flow fume hood. The vial was verified to contain live *Bacillus anthracis*.

An examination of Cao's background revealed no

terrorist activities. He had not visited any foreign countries since his immigration and none of his computer files or email records showed any illicit activity. There were no ties to Al Qaeda or any known terrorist groups. The FBI was concerned that Cao made frequent visits to New York City before and the day after the 9-11 attacks. But many of his friends and acquaintances verified that he was seeing Nancy who died in the attack. His mother was brought in and interrogated. When questioned about why he retained the lone anthrax-containing vial, he showed them the research experiments that he was planning. Although he went against his advisor's request to destroy these samples, Dr. Guowei nevertheless vouched for his student. After retaining Cao for several weeks, and at the approval of the Attorney General, all charges were dropped. Cao returned to the University to complete his studies. He was told to discontinue his work with anthrax.

Cao completed his studies and earned a master's degree. Professor Guowei encouraged him to continue on to get his doctorate. Cao was offered a teaching assistantship and accepted. Cao met a Korean girl, Ming in one of his classes and began dating her after the end of the semester. Within a year, she moved in with Cao. About six months later, Dr. Guowei asked Cao to attend a 5-day scientific conference. Ming had classes to attend and stayed behind. On a Saturday night, she was in her apartment fixing dinner for herself. She stir-fried some chicken but they were out of cooking sauce and seasoning. Looking in the very back of the refrigerator, she found a bottle labeled, "Cao's special sauce." Cao did most of the cooking when they ate at home. She knew this would probably taste good so she dumped the contents of the vial onto her food and ate it. Within a few hours, she started experiencing nausea, sore throat and a fever. It was the flu season so she thought that bed rest would be sufficient. When she didn't improve after two days, she called an ambulance and they took her to the hospital.

Cao came home on Thursday to find that Ming was not home. There was a message on the answering machine from Ming stating that she was sick and went to the hospital. When Cao entered the kitchen, he noticed that Ming had the bottle of his special sauce on the countertop. Cao originally had five vials of anthrax in the lab, not four. Just before the federal agents had raided his lab, Cao took the last vial home and hid it in the woods near his apartment. After the investigators finished the search of his possessions, he took the vial, relabeled it as his special sauce, and put it into his freezer. Cao remembered that he recently moved the bottle to the refrigerator when he was defrosting the freezer and he forgot to move it back. Now, Ming may have been exposed due to this terrible mistake! He rushed to the hospital. When he arrived, he found out that Ming had.......

*

Bacillus anthracis is a soil-bourne gram-positive rod that exists as an endospore and can be found in the soil of the earth. It was discovered in 1875 by Robert Koch, a German scientist. It can infect domesticated farm animals that graze in the field. The spores are extremely stable and can remain viable for decades. Individuals at highest risk are those who work with animal products (wool or meat) or work in a microbiology research or clinical laboratory. A vaccine is available for individuals deemed to be at high risk. The vaccine was first developed by Louis Pasteur in 1881, which resulted in the near eradication of deaths caused by this bacterium. The American vaccine is cellular while the Russian version uses live spores. A small percentage of individuals exhibit a reaction to the vaccine after inoculation.

Bacillus anthracis in the powdered form can transmit an infection through inhalation. Endospores germinate at the site of entry where they can circulate via the blood and lymphatic system and proliferate in tissues and organs. An individual exposed to anthrax exhibits non-specific flu-like symptoms. Survival of an acute infection requires treatment as soon as possible with antibiotics penicillin and ciprofloxacin.

The real graduate student from which this story is based attended the Pathobiology Program at the University of Connecticut. He kept the anthrax vials and was one of the first to be charged under the newly signed Patriot Act. The student was exonerated from all charges. He did not have any other vials at his research lab or at home.

The attacks on citizens from anthrax sent through the U.S. mail have led to the implementation of a sophisticated surveillance program by the U.S. Postal Office for detecting Bacillus anthracis. Mail passes through a device where aerosols are captured and sent to a detector where the mail is tested for the bacterium's genetic signature. Billions of pieces of mail have been screened with no incidents to date. Hooray for the U.S.P.O.!

Residency Termination

Marek Tauter grew up in the capital city of the Gabba Tutu Islands in the South Pacific. His father was a wealthy importer/exporter who would travel around the world to find unique items to sell. Marek was used to a life of privilege. He was a quiet boy, who studied a lot and loved to read. He was not like the other boys; all they wanted to do was play football in the fields. He preferred to go out into those fields to study nature and its wonders. He would dissect dead animals and insects that he found instead of kicking a stupid ball around. Marek did not have any friends in school, and didn't go on dates with girls, although he was not gay. His only hobby was target shooting with a pistol. Since his father was a wealthy man in a poor country, he needed armed bodyguards. They showed Marek how to use guns, and he would imagine shooting some of the bigger kids who bullied him in school. Marek was motivated to get into a good medical school and desperately wanted to leave the Islands. There was so much poverty, so many problems, and just too many ignorant natives. He had a private tutor from the U.K. who taught him the King's English. This greatly expanded his options.

Marek finished at the top of his high school graduating class. Through the help of his father's friend, he was accepted into a prestigious medical school in London. This school had a special accelerated program that enabled him to get a bachelor's and medical degrees in just six years.

Marek thrived at this school. He was finally at a place where there were plenty of intellectuals like him. Once there, he focused on his next goal. He had no interest in seeing patients and listening to their tiresome complaints. Psychiatry was not an option for the same reason. He hated children, so pediatrics was out. Because of a degenerative retinal disease, he could not be a surgeon although he felt he shared a bond with many of them since they were just as arrogant as he was. He also didn't have a high opinion of women. He felt superior to them and had little use for females in his medical school class. *They are there because somebody has to deliver the babies*, he thought to himself.

He knew he wanted to do research and find new medical knowledge. To be an expert in a field. To be recognized as a scholar. He felt that the medical field that was best suited to his needs was pathology. In order to prepare for a lifetime in research, Marek entered a Ph.D. program soon after his M.D. degree so he could learn how to do medical research and how to write research grants. He selected microbiology as his subspecialty. He completed his doctorate degree two years after starting. His Ph.D. thesis was on the routes of the transmission of *Rickettsia*, an infectious bacterium. Marek was now ready to choose a residency program.

Marek carefully studied his options. He had never been to the United States. He felt this was his best option for the future. In order to get accepted into a U.S. residency program, he knew he had to do well with the Educational Commission for

Foreign Medical Graduates Exam, a test to assess the readiness of international medical graduates to enter residency in the U.S. He also completed Steps 1 and 2 of the U.S. Medical License Examination, a requirement for American and foreign medical students alike. In preparing for these exams, he enrolled in online courses and took mock examinations.

Sometimes when he got a question wrong, he would think to himself, *I have new information that makes this answer wrong today. How can I do well on a test that has antiquated questions written by out-of-date educators who haven't done any research in decades? I guess I'll just have to select the commonly accepted "dumbed-down answer" approach.* But it didn't matter; Marek did very well on all of these exams. He knew he was ready to tackle a new world. But was the world ready for him?

The next step was to apply for the National Resident Matching Program, or simply, the "Match." Marek was invited to interview at six different pathology residency programs in the U.S. They were all the top programs in the country. Having a Ph.D. in a field related to pathology gave him an edge over the other students. Once he received his interview schedule in advance by email, he spent a good deal of time reviewing the research interests of each professor. He read and studied their recent publications. During the interviews, he asked probative and highly provocative questions about their work. While he knew he was smarter than any of them, he had to be careful not to display his huge ego. He was a clever manipulator. Even though he hated people, he recognized that he needed them to get where he was going.

At the end of the interview season for the Match, he and

the other candidates ranked the schools that they wanted most. The individual residency programs also ranked the students in their order of priority. Each school had a certain number of vacant positions. An individual whose priority ranking matched that of a school's was automatically offered admission. If a program had an opening without a matched student, the school would have to scramble to find someone who did not match any program or were, for some reason, not listed on the Match itself. A school's reputation would be downgraded if it had unfilled slots. If students didn't match, they would have to find programs with extra, unfilled slots.

On the day of the match, Marek saw a fellow student crying in the hall. Her printed Match result was in her hand. She was denied entry into a pediatrics programs, one of the more competitive residencies.

"What am I going to do now?" she said to Marek. "Pediatrics is the only thing I want to do."

"Do a year in another field and then transfer to peds," he told her. But what he really thought was that she had no chance. She was near the bottom of her class. But she was a caring person who really liked children. Marek thought to himself, *we have no need for compassion in this field. This is a serious science.* Marek left the building and didn't think about her again.

Dr. Marek Tauter was granted admission to a school in California that was ranked among the top three of all pathology training programs on the West Coast. It was his top choice and he couldn't wait to start. He was going to show them the next great Nobel Prize winner in medicine. Marek arrived on campus a week early to find an apartment, buy a car, and take part in orientation, including tours of the facility.

"What a waste of time," he said to his landlord. "I'm going to spend the next four years with these jerks. Why should I cow-tow to them earlier than I have to?" But he attended the orientation, said little to anyone, ate the hors d'oeuvres, and left the various gatherings at the earliest opportunity.

When the residency program finally began, the schedule of rotations for each resident was arranged and posted by the senior resident. The "SR" was selected by the faculty as the most outstanding resident in the senior class.

Having met all of the incoming residents, Marek thought, *no question, I'll be the SR in a few years.* The pathology residency program was broken down into anatomic and clinical pathology. Two years in each. Anatomic pathology included surgical pathology, cytology, and the autopsy service. Clinical pathology included chemistry, microbiology, hematology, and the blood bank. As he thought of each rotation, Marek wrote on the schedule what he thought about them.

Surgical path: *I'll master this subject in 3 weeks, tops.*

Cytology: *Who cares about PAP smears? That's for women.*

Autopsy: *Dumb. They're dead. Can't help 'um.*

Microbiology: *I could teach this better than they can.*

Blood bank: *Medical degree to dispense blood? A pharmacist should be doing this.*

The training schedule allowed time for elective rotations. Residents could select sub-specialty training in specific areas of interest, go to outside hospitals to gain perspective on how other labs operate, or conduct research. Marek knew that he would be conducting research.

*

Dr. Tautoru's first rotation was with me in the chemistry lab. Most of my residents were not interested in pursuing clinical chemistry as a final career objective. The day-to-day activity in the chemistry lab involved managing financial and personnel resources, biomedical engineering, and information technology. One of my residents once told me, "I didn't go to medical school to be an industrial process manager." Some residents were intimidated by the chemistry lab, because as an undergraduate student some years ago now, it might have been their worst science subject. The majority of them entered the field of pathology to signout biopsy specimens, not run laboratories. Invariably, they would take their vacation sometime during the third-month rotation. Most of my residents were ready to move on when the rotation was over, but at least they wanted to learn and were cordial. Marek, however, was an exception. After a few weeks, he told me that my rotation was stupid and worthless.

"In most hospitals, the lab is run by the senior technologist," Marek remarked. "They keep the trains operating and running on schedule," he said, meaning that the instruments needed to be functional 24 hours a day and results had to meet targeted turnaround time. "But they don't need a highly trained physician like me. I have more important things to do with my time."

Marek was absent during the rotation much of the time. When he was present, he was very arrogant to the technical staff. When he received a complaint from one of the doctors about a late test result, he would berate the laboratory individual involved. After the second time that happened, I met with Marek behind his closed office door.

"This is unprofessional behavior and I won't tolerate it. I know you don't care about chemistry, but I will not have you disrupt my service. You will apologize to the individuals involved, and if I see a repeat of this, I will throw you off the rotation. Without a satisfactory completion of clinical chemistry, you will not graduate."

Marek was regretful, not because of his behavior but because he'd let his ego get the best of him. He realized that this was not the way to be successful. For the remainder of the rotation, he was a model resident. He and I rarely spoke unless absolutely necessary.

Marek's next rotation was the clinical microbiology laboratory. He vowed to himself, *this rotation is going to be different. I'll pretend to be interested and to be learning something, but in reality, I will begin doing my real job—research.*

Dr. Georgio Rotunno was Italian and had trained in Rome as a microbiologist. Georgio's specialty was the study of antibiotic-resistant microorganisms. The National Institutes of Health funded his research studies. Georgio had been at the General Hospital for 20 years and had an outstanding record as a clinician, research scientist, and educator. Georgio had a wife and three teenage children, who, having been born in the U.S., were completely westernized, with no hint of an Italian accent. Georgio, on the other hand, still spoke like the first-generation immigrant that he was. Marek, not an American himself, found that refreshing. Georgio had played soccer when he was in school and he'd coached several of his kids' teams. His oldest son was now captain of his high school team. Whenever he was in town,

Georgio never missed attending a game.

Dr. Rotunno had read parts of Marek's Ph.D. thesis during his Match interview, and was largely responsible for the Department's high priority listing that had resulted in Marek matching the General's residency program. Now Georgio was impressed with Marek's knowledge and motivation in microbiology. Marek was able to handle his tasks efficiently and he worked hard during his rotation, this time without complaints from the section chief.

After one month on the rotation, Georgio asked Marek to consider doing research in an area of Georgio's expertise. Marek jumped at the chance. He saw Dr. Rotunno as the key to his future. Even after his mandatory rotation, Marek continued to work on the research project assigned to him by Georgio. He worked nights, weekends, even holidays. Satisfied with his level of progress and knowledge, Dr. Rotunno instructed Marek to design an experiment that would explain how a particular strain of bacteria mutated to become resistant to a commonly used antibiotic. Marek studied the literature, spoke to some experts over the phone and through email exchanges, and came up with a research plan. Dr. Rotunno thought the idea was unconventional and somewhat far-fetched but agreed to support the work.

Marek spent the next six months testing his theory, while simultaneously rotating through the blood bank and hematology. When he finished his research, he presented his work to Dr. Rotunno. Impressed with the findings, Georgio asked if Marek would be interested in presenting his work at the national microbiology meeting. Marek was thrilled. He prepared an abstract and the two doctors submitted it together, with Marek as the lead and Georgio as the senior author. Two months later, Marek received a letter indicating that his work was accepted for presentation. At this meeting, most of the abstracts were approved for presentation as a "poster"; the researcher would prepare his work in the form of a written display, and at the appointed time interval during the conference, would stand by the poster to meet other interested investigators to discuss the work. Those researchers with more highly rated abstracts, as deemed by a committee, were invited to give their work in the form of an oral presentation. Marek's abstract was selected to be one of the oral lectures. He and the others in this category were each allowed 12 minutes with three minutes allotted for questions by the audience.

What Dr. Rotunno didn't know was that Marek's study had actually failed to prove the mechanism for drug resistance. In fact, his theory was incorrect. Marek had undertaken additional studies to salvage his hypotheses but without success. He had never before failed at anything, and was devastated. He couldn't face Dr. Rotunno and tell him that his thinking was wrong. So he'd opened his spreadsheet containing the results of his experiments and reversed some of the findings so that they would match his hypothesis.

Dr. Rotunno is not smart enough to know what I did, he told himself. Four months later, when it was time to present the work to a national audience, there was a lot of buzz about it. After Marek's talk, many scientists went up to the podium to congratulate him for his study. Some of them were skeptical about his conclusions and said they were going to go back to their labs to try to duplicate his experiments. Marek didn't know that this was standard practice in clinical research. He thought that they would just accept his conclusions as gospel and move on to other topics. His work had never been challenged before in his young career. And by then, he'd convinced himself that his own fabrication was the truth.

*

The following year, Dr. Tautoru began his training in surgical pathology. He found out quickly that he had been wrong about how simple this work was. The pathologists kept him busy until 8:00 or 9:00 p.m. each night, so he had little time to think about his microbiology research. He actually learned a lot about pathology and was humbled by it. Residents often spent two additional years doing a surgical pathology fellowship in order to master this discipline. Marek learned enough to know that surgical pathology was not for him. *The pathologists are too consumed in signing out cases for them to do any real research*, he reasoned to himself.

Meanwhile, during this next year, Dr. Rotunno started getting messages about Marek's research. None of his colleagues had been able to duplicate the work. They all had gotten results that were just the opposite of what Marek had reported. Georgio went back to the lab and accessed the original data that was still on Marek's computer there. He compared the raw data generated by the instrument Marek used against the statistical files used to generate his conclusions. The data entered into the statistics program had been reversed. Could this have been an honest mistake? Could there have been a computer glitch somewhere? Suspecting the worst, he went to the department's computer geek to find out.

Tommy Smith was a master of recovering erased files from hard drives. Tommy had learned how to do this during an internship with the Central Intelligence Agency. He had a brief career as a forensic information technologist. But he didn't like all of the cloak and dagger, so he joined the pathology department. He knew that unless the drive had been reformatted, he'd be able to retrieve much, if not all, of Marek's files, even if he'd deleted them from his computer's recycle bin. Marek had made a copy of his data files, altered the copy, and then erased the original. If he had simply changed the original file, the recovery would not have been possible. After a day, Tommy emailed the recovered original file to Dr. Rotunno. It had not been overwritten by other data.

"I don't know what it means, Doc, but here are the original data files," Tommy wrote in his email with the data attached. Georgio also found out that the instrument Marek had used automatically populated the results directly into the statistical software. The data showed that Marek's original conclusion was the same one that Georgio's colleagues had come to: that Dr. Tautoru's theory was proven false. But then Marek had created a later file where the exact same data were reversed. Georgio went back to the instrument files to see if new experiments had been done that coincided with the creation of this file. He found none. Georgio concluded that Marek had falsified his findings.

Horrified, Dr. Rotunno called Marek to schedule a meeting in his office that afternoon. He told Marek that something was wrong with his research data. Marek knew that a disclosure that he falsified data could ruin his young career. Over his lunch hour, Marek went home, found the hand gun that he'd had since childhood, and went into Dr. Rotunno's office.

I was in my office down the hall from Georgio's eating my lunch. I saw Marek walk past my office, but thought nothing of it. I was opening my mail when I heard a loud crack. But it was a clear and sunny day so it couldn't be thunder. The noise came from Georgio's office. I dropped my sandwich and letter opener and rushed in the direction of the shot. Georgio's office door was open and Marek was standing there holding the firearm. Marek was in shock and didn't move. Dr. Rotunno was slumped in his chair. Blood was rushing onto the carpet. In Dr. Rotunno's hand was a notice of an investigation for research fraud that he had filed with the school's research compliance office. It was his duty to report this since his work was federally funded. He was just about to issue this summons. I carefully took the gun out of Marek's hand. He did not respond. He had a blank stare on his face.

Marek Tautoru was convicted of second degree murder. The jury determined that his actions were not premeditated. He just wanted to frighten Dr. Rotunno, but he snapped when he saw the termination letter. Marek was sentenced to 8 years and was put under psychiatric care. The department at General Hospital established a memorial scholarship in Dr. Georgio Rotunno's name. Each year, a deserving resident would be awarded a modest stipend to conduct clinical research in the department. Georgio's family attended the inaugural award ceremony. I gave a short speech in remembrance of Dr. Rotunno.

This was the third case of murder or manslaughter to

occur among the various departments I have been involved with. Cao Pham was indicted for the voluntary manslaughter of his girlfriend when she died of an anthrax poisoning. And then there was the Calvin, whose family died at the hands of a drug intoxicated driver. Calvin was my toxicology manager who left after their deaths, only to purse profit at the expense and misery of others.

*

The diminishing availability of federal funding for conducting research, and the pressure of university faculty promotion and tenure that require independent financial support, have led to an increasing incidence of fraud among investigators in recent years. The National Institutes of Health's Office of Management Assessment has a standard operating procedure for reporting fraud, waste, and abuse by grantees. The Office of Inspector General oversees abuse by contractors. Anyone involved with a grant can anonymously report an abuse to these offices, triggering a financial audit or peer review of scientific findings. Penalties for organizations and individuals convicted of these offenses include revocation of funding, fines to the investigator or institution, and imprisonment of guilty individuals. Recently, Cornell University settled a fraud lawsuit by repaying $2.6 million back to the NIH. This case was based on the lack of full disclosure of pre-existing funding by researchers.

There are also regulations surrounding investigator responsibilities for industry-sponsored clinical trials. It is a conflict of interest for a principal investigator to participate in a trial when he or she has personal financial assets in the study sponsor, such as salary, stocks, or stock options. It is possible that the researcher may bias the outcome of a study in favor of the sponsor, thereby personally benefiting from the company's future income. The research or clinician must recognize that

195

the purpose of the pharmaceutical industry and companies that make diagnostic equipment, devices, or laboratory tests is financial gain, while the physician or scientist must only be concerned with scientific truth and healthcare improvement.

Dr. Rotunno's downfall was caused by not regularly checking on his student's work. He trusted that Marek was doing his studies objectively and without bias. As an active clinical researcher, I cannot put too much fault with Dr. Rotunno's actions. These residents are not undergraduate or graduate students but professionals with medical degrees. We expect that they will not need as much personal direction as they may have earlier in their careers.

Moreover, clinical scientists, unlike basic science researchers, have the added responsibility of patient care, or in Georgio's case, his clinical laboratory. Therefore it is exceptionally difficult to get federal funding when one can only devote part of their professional time to research. Recognizing this, the National Institutes of Health has instituted a program to encourage more research by physician scientists. A component of this program is the "buy down" of a doctor's time away from clinical responsibilities in order to do research.

The real student on whom this story is based was a pathology resident at the University of Washington in June of 2000. The resident, distraught at being dismissed from the program, fired four shots from a pistol and killed Dr. Rodger Haggitt, a renowned gastrointestinal pathologist. The student, Dr. Jian Chen then turned the gun on himself.

Consent

Our medical technology training program involves exposing our students to the clinical practice of laboratory medicine, as well as research studies and clinical trials that are ongoing in my laboratory. For most physicians and lay personnel, when someone says or if it is stated in an advertisement that this product has been verified in a "clinical trial, " it normally means that a research study was conducted to determine the clinical benefits of a product, whether it is a drug or medical device. Such statements made on product advertisements are meant to give more credence and add greater marketing value to the product.

In the clinical laboratory, trials are also needed for products to be used on patient's blood or other biological samples. These trials document the purpose and value of laboratory information that a doctor can use to diagnose, treat and in some cases, predict clinical outcomes based on a laboratory test. One of the trials we conducted a few years ago involved collection of an extra tube of blood so that we can evaluate a new test for heart disease. The protocol was submitted to our university's "Institutional Review Board (IRB)" where Board members decided if the benefits for those who agree to participate in the trial outweigh the risks. The "benefits" might not be in the patient's current medical care, but might influence their future treatment. Alternately, benefits can be defined as advancement in medical sciences as a whole. These are some of the issues that the IRB consider.

Clinical trials involving pharmaceutical agents and medical devices are carefully conducted to determine a drug's efficacy and safety profile. Drugs can produce adverse side effects and even death without any warning. Therefore regulatory agencies such as the Food and Drug Administration play an essential role in protecting patients from untoward harm. Sales and marketing of these drugs cannot commence without such regulatory approval.

A similar situation exists regarding in vitro diagnostic (IVD) laboratory tests. Clinical laboratory tests are designed to produce medical information that is used by doctors to manage their patients. The tests themselves do not cause harm, however, incorrect results can mislead a physician to use the wrong medication or therapy. Because of this potential danger, the FDA also regulates most laboratory tests and the instruments that generate lab test results. New lab tests must be studied in a clinical trial. Results must provide medical information that is equal to or better than the existing test in current use. Naturally, tests that produce inferior results are not likely approved by the FDA.

A consistent component to most clinical trials for IVD involves the collection of extra blood specimens to be tested by the experimental device. Taking blood outside of the context of the patient's medical care is considered invasive and requires written consent by the potential donor. Recently, I had a discussion of this topic with one of my students, Justin Forza. The study sponsor had requested that we withdraw a small amount of extra blood at the same time that a venipuncture was being performed for the patient's routine medical care.

"Why do we have to get permission to collect just a few drops of extra blood?" he asked. "We're only taking one teaspoon. You told us that a normal sized man has more than 5 quarts of blood," Justin stated. "Certainly he will not miss the small amount. Isn't the issue the needle stick itself and not the few extra drops of blood taken?"

"Since the blood is not for their immediate medical care, we still have to ask, however little we need. We would even need to ask permission to obtain urine, even though we excrete this everyday," I explained.

"But this makes no sense. We always collect more blood than we use and discard the remainder. Why is that OK?"

I responded, "The extra blood that we take is to make sure we have enough for our testing. We collect extra in case we have to repeat a test in order to get the right answer."

"Could we use this extra blood that is scheduled for discard instead of asking for more?" Justin asked.

"We often do this, but most of the time, we also need some medical information from the patient, and need the patient's permission to look at their private medical record. Only in situations where it would be difficult or impossible to consent the patient can we get permission from our IRB committee to use leftover blood without permission," I said.

Justin was still confused. "But you as the head of the laboratory have permission to examine medical records anyways. How is this different?"

"In the context of providing medical care to our patients, that is true. Our access to a patient's medical chart is sometimes necessary in the proper interpretation of our laboratory results. But this permission does not extend to conducting medical research. So when I look at medical records, I have to be sure I am doing it for the right purpose," I explained. "Our access is regularly audited by our privacy office to ensure that it is appropriate and necessary. There have been cases where access was inappropriately acquired by healthcare personnel, and resulted in significant disciplinary action by the offender."

"Can you tell me when this happened?" Justin asked.

"Do you know Farrah Fawcett, the hot blond from Charlie's Angels?" I asked.

"You mean Drew Barrymore" Justin responded.

"No, there was a TV show and Farrah was on it. Anyways, she developed anal cancer and died in 2009 in Los Angeles. Before she died, her medical records were accessed by an employee at UCLA who sold news of her cancer and other medical information to a newspaper tabloid. This case led to the passage of stiffer privacy laws and higher penalties for the breech of medical information," I concluded.

Getting back to the original topic, Justin asked, "So the need to obtain patient consent to access medical information stems from Farrah's case?"

I said, "No, the process of informed consent was created several decades before her death........."

*

Satchel was a slave to the Stubbs family in rural Alabama. He and his children worked the cotton fields for 12 or more hours every day. After the South lost the War Between the States, Satchel and his family were declared free. The Stubbs family turned Satchel and other slaves into tenant farmers. A portion of each farmer's crop would be paid to the landlord. This practice went on for several generations.

One of Satchel's grandsons, Leroy Willis, was born a few years after the turn of the century. Neither he nor any of his generation of boys and girls received much formal education, and Leroy was illiterate. This lack of education may have been a means by the Stubbs family to keep their former male slaves as servants to the land and females as maids to their plantation.

Unlike his brothers, sisters, and cousins, Leroy did not want to work the fields his whole life. When he was 20, he left home and he took a job as a gas station attendant in the small town of Tuskegee, Alabama. Almost all of the residents of this town were black. Leroy had no trouble fitting in. Over the years, he learned how to make minor repairs on automobiles. Leroy never married, but he had more than his share of girlfriends and female acquaintances. While in his late-thirties, Leroy contracted a venereal disease. His body was full of sores and rashes including a chancre on his penis. The lesion was painless and he continued to have intercourse with female partners. After a few more weeks, he went to the Tuskegee General Hospital. His doctors were more than familiar with these presenting signs and symptoms.

"Have you been with a lot of women?" was one of the first questions that Cedric Brown, one of the doctors in the clinic, asked.

"Yes sir. I gave them a little of hooch and we have a grand old time," Leroy said. Although Prohibition ended in 1933 with the repealed in 18th Amendment, Leroy continued to get bootleg alcohol from neighbors and friends, some 8 years later.

"You have bad blood," the doctor said. He really didn't know what was causing this illness.

"You got anything to give me for this," Leroy asked.

"There are some white doctors in town right now that can help," the doctor said.

"How much is this gonna cost, 'cause I don't have much money" Leroy said.

"There is some kind of study that the government is paying for. It ain't going to cost you nothin," replied the doctor.

*

Dr. Denis Cypress was a senior scientist from the U.S. Public Health Service and the principal investigator for the Tuskegee Syphilis Study. This study was initiated in 1932 with the objective of studying the long-term medical effects of individuals with this infection. Dr. Cypress and his co-workers hoped to understand and map the natural history of the disease so that when drugs were available, they could be used at the appropriate time. Dr. Brown contacted Dr. Cypress telling him that he had a patient that might qualify for the Syphilis Study. Dr. Cypress met with Leroy the following week.

"We are going to give you pills that will help treat your bad blood," he told Leroy.

"Are them pills going to fix me up?" Leroy asked.

"They are just what you need," Dr. Cypress said. The

investigator did not mention to Leroy th
made of sugar and they had no effectiv
won't hurt this poor boy, he thought to l
about this disease that can help future patients.

Leroy agreed to be a subject of their work. He
some pills each month that he was to take and was subjected to a
medical and physical exam on a regular basis. The treatment
appeared to work at first, and his rash diminished somewhat.
Leroy felt better and thought he would be back to his old self. In
reality, Leroy's initial medical success was due to the well known
"placebo effect." He believed that these pills would help him, and
his body and mind responded appropriately. But over the
ensuing years, his symptoms got worse. He started to suffer from
neurologic symptoms including weakness, headache, and
muscular aches. He was no longer able to work and became a
ward of the state.

*

A few years later, penicillin was discovered to be a useful
treatment for syphilis, although it wasn't immediately available at
the Tuskegee General Hospital. Dr. Cypress became attached to
several of his patients and pleaded with the Public Health Service
to allow him to withdraw his patients from the study and treat his
men with the antibiotic. But the administrators told him that the
information gathered by these participants was so valuable that it
outweighed the small chance that these men would be cured
during these later stages of the infection. So Leroy and many
other men from Tuskegee were denied treatment. They were not
told that drugs were available. Dr. Cypress believed this was
wrong but the principal investigators of the study would not

discovered. Syphilis is transmitted through sex, or from an infected mother to child. The incidence of syphilis is higher in developing countries, among gay men, and prostitutes. There is no vaccine available to protect the population. The use of condoms during sexual intercourse can diminish the spread of the disease.

A total of 399 black men from rural Alabama were recruited as subjects for the Tuskegee Syphilis Study from 1932 and 1972. Like Leroy, most were poor and uneducated. Published research reports appeared every several years in reputable medical journals. Although lesser known in history, the U.S. also conducted syphilitic studies in Guatemala from 1946 to 1948.

The abuse of subjects in the Tuskegee Syphilis Study led to the publication of the Belmont Report in 1978. This document led to the creation of the Office of Human Protections sometimes termed "Institutional Review Board or IRB." Today, all research conducted on human subjects is reviewed and approved by the IRB, a group of physicians, ethicists, and members of the lay public. All medical centers and hospitals conducting human research have IRBs. They oversee protocols to determine if human medical research is conducted in an ethical manner. Participation must be voluntary, and occur without undue coercion, particularly vulnerable groups, such as children, prisoners, or individuals who do not understand the objectives of the research study. The informed consent document is critical for conducting medical research studies. This document informs potential participants of the study objective, their role, risks associated with participation, provision for medical care for injuries or diseases caused by the study, and a means to withdraw from a study at any time. Leroy Willis was not informed of the objectives of the study and was not told of alternative medications available after his enrollment. It was clearly an exploitation of a vulnerable population. As a member of a minority race living in America, I cannot comprehend how scientists and physicians, with all good intentions, could have willingly permitted this practice.

Bad Breath

****

As an advertising executive, Connor Geiger was a driven man. He had an office overlooking Madison Avenue in Midtown Manhattan. As far as he was concerned, the office could have easily been in Manhattan, Kansas. Connor rarely looked out the window of his office to enjoy the view of that bustling city. One Saturday at his home in suburban Connecticut town, he had this recurrent discussion with his wife.

"It is the nature of my profession," he told his wife Marie. "I have to prove my worth every day."

"But your last ad campaign for the soup company made them millions of dollars," Marie remarked. "Doesn't that prove your worth?"

"There is a sign in the office that we all work by. It states, 'What have you done for us lately?'" Connor replied.

"You're working yourself into an early grave. Just like your father," Marie said as she left the room. She loved him dearly but there was nothing she could do to get him to slow down. His job was his mistress.

Connor's father died of a heart attack at the early age of 52 years. Like Connor, his father was an executive in an insurance company in Hartford and was also a workaholic. Connor's dad did not have high cholesterol or premature hardening of the arteries. His death was attributed to "excessive stress."

Connor worked 10 hour days for five days a week. He took the train in from their home and was in the office by 7 am. He was always in a rush and usually skipped breakfast. He carried his briefcase with him at all times and worked while commuting. It would be another 20 years before cell phones were in widespread use, otherwise, had they been available, he would have been constantly on it talking to clients and office associates. The minute he walked into the office, his secretary would have coffee waiting for him. He drank 4-5 cups during the day, always black. Connor's lunch habits were also poor. He ate at fast food restaurants because he didn't want to take time away from the job. When he did go out with colleagues and clients, they often went to a Thai restaurant, where Connor ordered dishes that were hot and spicy. Connor was also a chain smoker. He went through an entire pack of unfiltered cigarettes each day. At the end of the workday, he would sometimes go to a bar near the office before going home. Connor was not an alcoholic, but a shot or two of bourbon would take the edge off the day. On weekends, Connor would play golf at the local country club. This was his only means of exercise. But he rode in a golf cart and never walked the course. During his round, he would smoke several large cigars.

It was somewhat predictable that Connor developed a stomach ulcer while he was in his mid-forties. He went to see Dr. John Bennett, who was his family physician. Dr. Bennett told

Connor that stress, smoking, drinking, and poor diet were responsible for his ulcer.

"Did your father have ulcers?" he asked Connor during a routine visit. Connor nodded yes. "Your genetics may be an additional factor in explaining why you developed this ulcer. Excess acid in your stomach is eroding the protective lining of your digestive system. I am going to prescribe antacids that will neutralize your stomach acid and relieve your pain." The antacid treatment was not successful in eradicating Connor's ulcer. For many years, he suffered from stomach cramps, nausea, bloating, and black stools caused from bleeding in the gastrointestinal tract that led to the production of hemoglobin release into his feces. At the advice of his doctor, Connor scaled back on his work schedule, stopped smoking and drinking alcohol. A few years later, Dr. Bennett read about a new theory regarding the etiology of gastric ulcers. He asked Connor to come back to the office where he underwent a new laboratory test...

*

Dr. Martin Barry received his doctoral degree in internal medicine and underwent residency and fellowship training at the University Hospital in the early 1980s. There, he met Adelaide Kilgore, a young pathologist who was also in training. They dated for a while but later decided to be just friends and colleagues. Both Martin and Adelaide had an interest in gastrointestinal diseases. Adelaide was studying stomach biopsies and noticed that some had bacteria that appeared to be "curved." Martin then suggested that these bacteria could be the cause of peptic ulcers.

"Nonsense," was Adelaide's response. "It is well established that the harsh acidic media of the stomach is the responsible cause. These are curious but probably incidental findings."

"But I just read a paper that described *Campylobacter jejuni* as a cause of food-borne gastroenteritis" Martin said.

"*Campylobacter* is not the only microorganism that has a flagella." They both new that a flagella is a hair like structure that protrudes out of bacteria and parasites. "Have you considered *Helicobacter?*"

That conversation launched a new area of investigation by the two scientists/clinicians. In reviewing the literature, Martin found case reports where spiral-shaped bacteria were seen in gastric fluids but nobody thought that this was the causative agent. They spent the next two years characterizing stomach biopsies of patients with gastric ulcers. They found that this bacterium was prevalent in affected patients, but did not see it in patients with other causes of abdominal pain with bleeding ulcers, such as food poisoning.

Martin and Adelaide submitted a manuscript to a high ranking gastrointestinal journal on their clinical observations and hypothesis that *Helicobacter* is a causative agent in gastric ulcers. The paper was rejected by three expert reviewers whose names were blinded to the authors. In the reviewer comments, there were adjectives like, "unsubstantiated conclusions," "irresponsible speculation," and "sensationalist journalism." Martin and Adelaide were crushed to see their work so thoroughly dismissed. Undaunted, they sent it to a clinical microbiology journal following some minor editing to match the journal's publication style. Within a few weeks, more rejection letters returned. These letters, however, were less critical and more supportive. There was one comment that was particularly helpful. "These authors have not fulfilled Koch's postulate to establish a causative relationship between a microbe and disease." Martin asked Adelaide what she knew about Koch. Adelaide, being still rather junior in the field of microbiology, was nevertheless embarrassed that she didn't consider the importance of this key postulate in formulating their work.

"In 1890, Koch, a German microbiologist studying cholera and tuberculosis listed four postulates. In the first two, the microorganism must be found in abundance and can be isolated from a diseased patient and not found in healthy subjects. We have shown this," Adelaide said. "But in the last two, the cultured microorganism must cause disease when introduced into a healthy individual and the microorganism re-isolated from the diseased experimental host. We need to find an animal model to see if we can infect it with *Helicobacter*," was Adelaide's concluding statement.

For the next 6 months, the two acquired numerous mammalian species, infected them with *Helicobacter* and waited for the presence of a gastric ulcer. Their studies were conducted in mice, rats, rabbits, and piglets. None of them harbored the bacterium. Martin thought to himself, *maybe all of the reviewers were right and we are wrong.* Many of Martin's colleagues were now assistant professors at major medical universities or had thriving medical practices. Martin was still just a research scientist and paid at a rather low salary. *Have I wasted the last 3 years of my life?* Martin went home to his wife, Mary, whom he married two years earlier. They were hoping to start a family but could not afford children on their combined salary. Mary worked as a cashier at a neighborhood grocery store and together, they barely made ends meet. Martin asked her if he should stop this line of research and accept an offer he received a year earlier to join a group of general practice physicians.

"Do you still believe that your theory is correct?" Mary asked her husband.

"Yes, but I can't prove it, but I know in my heart that this is correct," he said to her.

"But why are you so sure?" she asked.

"I have begun giving broad spectrum antibiotics to some of the clinic's patients who have gastric ulcers. Many of these patients got better. I am sure that it because the drugs are killing the bacteria" Martin disclosed to his wife.

"Was that ethical?" where her next question.

"Giving an antibiotic to someone who has flu like symptoms is not out of bounds. I just don't know if the drugs are treating the ulcer or a bacterial infection."

"Give your research a little more time. We have enough money to live on. I can ask my parents for some support if we need to," Mary said.

While Martin was happy that Mary was so supportive, he did not like the idea of asking her parents for support. While Mary's folks liked Martin, he sensed that they would have preferred that she had married the son of a long-time family friend. So Martin set a deadline for himself to find the proof he needed. He and Adelaide tried a few more animal models but to no avail. The research funds that he was given to perform this project was drying up and he was reaching his self-imposed deadline. Martin concluded that this infection maybe unique to humans and that he needed a human guinea pig. Martin went back to the lab and had his research nurse perform an endoscopy procedure on him. He didn't tell the nurse what he was planning, just that he needed to reconfirm what a normal result looked like. The next day, when he was alone in the lab, Martin drank a solution containing live cultured *Helicobacter pylori!* Martin did not seek permission from the University's ethics committee nor did he tell his own wife. Within three days, he became sick with a bloody diarrhea and vomiting. He became anemic and weak due to blood loss from the ulcer. But he waited for a few more days before he told anyone. By then, his doctor admitted him to a hospital. He told the doctors that he had a gastric ulcer, and asked them for an endoscopy. A biopsy was performed and the diagnosis was confirmed. He arranged for the gastric specimen to be sent to his research lab for culturing. After a few days, his research laboratory confirmed the presence of *H. pylori*. Both his wife and Adelaide were at his hospital bed when he received the news that *H. pylori* were detected. His theory was proven correct. Elated by the news but exhausted by his illness, he hugged his wife and quietly mumbled to his lab partner:

"Koch. Koch. Post. Post-u-late. We now have, have parts 3 and, and 4." Then he passed out. When he awoke the next day, Martin learned that he was being treated with antibiotics. Martin denied that he was sick because he wanted the infection to take its full course. Fortunately, he made a full recovery from his self-inflected infection.

Martin presented his results at a national gastrointestinal disease conference. While many in the audience were appalled that he used himself as a subject, they began to give his theory credence. Within a year, he received funding to perform a prospective double blind study to see if antibiotics could cure stomach and duodenal ulcers. If *Helicobacter* causes ulcers, treated patients should have better outcomes. The study was conducted at multiple centers. When half of the targeted enrollments were achieved, an interim analysis was conducted. When the identities of the "treated" and "placebo groups" were unmasked, Martin and his collaborators saw that the patients treated with antibiotics had a significant improvement in outcomes. The data was discussed by members of the University's ethics committee, who determined that the trial was a success, and that it was no longer ethical to continue the trial to its planned conclusion. The rationale was that individuals receiving the placebo drug were not benefitting from the antibiotics given to the treated group. Years later, Martin and Adelaide were heralded worldwide for their medical discovery.

*

Within a few years of Martin and Adelaide's discovery on *H. pylori*, Connor was seen by a gastroenterologist at my hospital. We were experimenting with a new diagnostic procedure to diagnose a *H. pylori* infection. Connor was instructed to drink a solution containing a urea solution where the carbon atom was labeled with the ^{13}carbon isotope. This naturally occurring isotope is not radioactive, is very stable, and is found in all organic compounds with a 1% abundance. *Helicobacter* is known as a "urea-splitting" microorganism. If present in Connor's intestinal tract, the bacteria will produce urease, an enzyme that metabolizes the labeled urea producing labeled carbon dioxide as a byproduct. This gas is normally exhaled and can be detected in an infected patient's breath. The breath test requires the use of mass spectrometry, which examines the molecular weight of compounds. The use of the [13]carbon isotope will produce a CO_2 molecule that is one molecular mass unit larger than the usual gas that contains the [12]carbon atom.

A Mylar balloon was brought to the examination room. Connor was instructed to drink the solution spiked with [13]carbon. I assured him that exposure to this isotope was completely safe. After 30 and 60 minutes, Connor was told to exhale his breath into separate balloons. The opening of each was sealed and I delivered the sample to my mass spectrometer laboratory. The techs injected the gas directly from the balloon into the instrument and within seconds a peak for [13]CO_2 became apparent on the printout. This confirmed that Connor had a gastric ulcer caused by a *H. pylori* infection. When Dr. Bennett received the test result, he was immediately prescribed antibiotics. At the end of a one week course of the medication, Connor felt better than he had in years. A repeat breath test was negative indicating that his infection had been successfully treated. Connor went back to working full time as an advertising executive. Although the stress in his life was not the cause of his gastric infection, Connor led a much healthier life with no smoking, a better diet, shorter work hours, and more exercise.

*

The correlation between H. pylori *infection and ulcers was discovered by Dr. Barry Marshall and Robin Warren working at Royal Perth Hospital in Western Australia in 1982. For their discovery, the pair won the Nobel Prize in Physiology or Medicine in 2005. Dr. Marshall and Warren faced considerable scrutiny from their colleagues when their* theories were first published. When these scientists failed to find a suitable animal model, Dr. Marshall did self-inoculate himself with active Helicobacter *bacterium* in order to prove this theory. Within three days after Dr. Marshall drank a dish containing H. *Pylori*, his mother noticed that he developed halitosis, the scientific term for "bad breath." This was because his infection increased his gastric *pH*, resulting in an alteration of this gut flora. These bacteria produced gaseous waste products that were expelled through his breath. Performing human self-experimentation today violates regulations established by Institutional Review Boards and Human Ethics Committees. The publication of such results would not be possible.

Today, it is known that H. pylori infections are responsible for the majority of cases of gastric and duodenal ulcers. Approximately 50% of the world's population harbor H. *pylori* in their upper gastrointestinal tract, with the majority of these individuals showing no signs of an ulcer. It is not exactly known how the infection is transmitted, but it is thought to be due to contaminated food and water. As such, third-word countries have a higher incidence of infection than the Western world. Fortunately, the rate of infection is decreasing around the world. Gastric ulcers are treated with antibiotics such as clarithromycin and amoxicillin, and use of drugs known as proton pump inhibitors such as omeprazole. Proton pump inhibitors reduce the amount of acid secreted into the stomach. There have been recent reports of antibiotic-resistant H. pylori. Because of increased resistance issues, a sequential regimen of a proton pump inhibitor (PPi) plus amoicillin for 5 days then a PPi, clarithromycin, and tinidazole for 5 days is recommended. The cure rate is 90%.

Diagnosis of H. pylori infection can be accomplished by the carbon urea test or antigen testing on stool. The gold standard is a *gastric biopsy where a specimen is collected during endoscopy. Urea and a pH indicator are added to the biopsy. An increase in the pH, as signified by a change in the color of the indicator paper, confirms the infection, because ammonia is a weak base and is produced from the urease reaction.*

Epilogue

****

In my first book, *Toxicology! Because What You Don't Know Can Kill You*, I describe the bad outcomes that occur when people use drugs. The toxicology laboratory has special analytical tools that enable us to be detectives. Results of drug and alcohol tests often work their way into the courtroom. In my second book, *The Hidden Assassin. When Clinical Laboratory Test Go Awry*, people become sick or die indirectly through the absence of a clinical laboratory test, the inappropriate performance of the test or the wrong interpretation of a result.

In *Microbiology! Because What You Don't Know Will Kill You* relate to infections by bacteria, viruses, and parasites when unrecognized, can kill or make you seriously ill. The laboratory plays an important role in detection and selecting the appropriate therapy to treat the infection. But it is up to us to understand how we can get into trouble and what we can do to avoid it.

A secondary theme of this work is the illustration of the importance of microorganism to our daily health. Even in a healthy individual, the number of microorganisms in our bodies exceed the number of human cells by 10 to 1. Clearly, we could not exist without bacterial flora. It is highly ironic, therefore, that people who avoid contact with microbes are at greatest risk for an infection. The old saying, "possession is nine-tenths of the law" applies. Normal bacterial colonies are the best defense against invading pathogens. Without these "soldiers" manning the fort, the kingdom is ripe for an overthrow.

Other books by this author, available through:

www.alanhbwu.com

Toxicology! Because What You Don't Know Can Kill You.

Collection of short stories containing real toxicology cases.

<u>Online Reviews:</u>

I loved this book because of the short stories (I am a busy mom of 2 kids under the age of 4, so anything short and sweet is awesome). They were fascinating and captivating and very though provoking! I particularly loved that the stories made me outraged at some behavior and sympathetic at others. Things that I never imagined could happen were mortifying to read and that's what I found especially captivating about this book from cover to cover! If you want to have your eyes opened and mind blown, you're absolutely going to be hooked!

Dr. Wu is a combination of Sherlock Homes and Dr. Watson. This book is not only fun to read, but it is also educational. Although the science is complex, the author breaks it down so even a lay person such as myself can understand it. The short-story writing style makes it feel like a quick read and keeps you turning the pages to discover the twist at each unique ending.

The Hidden Assassin: When Clinical Lab Tests Go Awry

Collection of true short stories containing real clinical laboratory cases.

Online Reviews:

This book of true medical short stories is fascinating. It kept my interest one after another. I had no intention of reading them all in one day, when I started. But each one was suspenseful, short and to the point; many, many times with surprise endings. I believe in recommending it so enthusiastically that I have purchased two extras as loners for friends! Alan Wu definitely is among my top authors since this book.

Here, in Dr. Wu's second book in his newly-created genre of 'clinical lab tales' non-fiction, he expands the scope to include a wider variety of testing situations. The stories are gripping, and address an important need. There is a defacto veil of mutual ignorance between the vast majority of the public, who all too frequently know virtually nothing about the 'blood tests' their doctors order on them, and the countless laboratory workers involved behind the scenes in supporting their care, who (due to privacy laws and other valid reasons) almost never know much or anything about the lives of those they serve. This book provides both groups with a sample of what it would be like to have this veil lifted. On behalf of both groups, thank you once again.

Made in the USA
Columbia, SC
12 July 2018